Southern Comfort

SPECIAL EDITION

NATASHA MADISON

Becca without you there is no Southern Series!

Cover Design: Jay Aheer https://www.simplydefinedart.com/

Editing done by Jenny Sims Editing4Indies

Proofing Julie Deaton by Deaton Author Services https://www.facebook.
com/jdproofs/

One

"Hello?" I say after two rings, and then I want to kick myself when I realize I didn't even check to see who it was.

"You have a collect call from an inmate at ..." When the recorded message starts, I do what I've done the other fifty times and hang up. Closing my eyes, I take a deep breath and put down the phone.

"Why can't he just fucking leave me alone?" I wonder if this will ever end. Will he ever stop trying to call me? I've already called his lawyer and threatened to file a restraining order against him if he doesn't stop trying to contact me. His lawyer assured me that his client would stop. Surprise, he lied. It seems I was going to have to get my own lawyer and do what I needed to do for me. I put my hands on my face, and my stomach grumbles. Looking up to check the clock on the stove, I see it's after three. I've been sitting at Casey's island since this morning. I love working here. The windows make everything so bright that I almost feel like I'm outside. He even brought me wildflowers from the field the other day to bring color into the house.

1

"Shit, how did it get so late?" I've been working on the Christmas spread for the magazine. Since Kallie did not come over this morning, I just worked straight through. Standing, I walk over to the fridge and take out the plate of sandwiches that Charlotte delivered this morning along with fresh muffins. I also grab the bottle of wine and pour myself a glass. I'm not driving anywhere, and it's almost five o'clock. As I pick up the glass to take a drink, my phone rings again. I groan, but this time, I check who's calling first.

Cowboy.

"Hey there, cowboy," I say after I swipe to answer it.

"Hey, darlin'." His voice comes out smooth, and I smile, which is silly since I live with him, and I saw him three hours ago. "Whatcha doin'?" I've never actually lived with a man. I mean, I'm not living *living* with him since I sleep in my room and he sleeps in his. But we do share the kitchen and the living room, and he does walk around without a shirt, which wreaks havoc on my restraint. *He's just making sure you're safe, Olivia,* I keep reminding myself over and over.

"I'm just about to eat a sand—" I say with a smirk, and then something catches my attention out of the corner of my eye, and I stop talking. Looking over, I see a shadow on the back porch. I move my head to the side, hoping to get a glimpse of his face, but I only see a black jacket. I don't know why, but my senses go into overload. I'm sure it's nothing. Probably just my imagination playing games with me.

"Hello?" Casey says.

"Someone was at the back door." The words come out in a whisper, and my heart pounds. Then I turn back to where I saw the shadow, but nothing is there.

"What do you mean?" he asks, his voice tight now as I try to get my heart rate back to normal. But something isn't right, and I don't know what it is.

I turn and start to walk back. "I just saw a shadow at the

back door, and I was ..." But I stop when I feel eyes looking at me and turn to see beady eyes looking at me from the side window.

I scream out in fright and shock as the phone falls from my hand and the wine bottle that I forgot I was holding crashes to the floor and shatters. Looking down, I see the wine all over the floor around my feet, and then my eyes travel over to look at the phone and the picture of me and Casey lit up on the screen. When I look up again toward the window, I see him. He smiles at me, but nothing about his smile is friendly. Dressed in all black, he looks like he has his hair pulled back into a ponytail and a scar across his cheek. He screams evil, and when my mind finally places him, I gasp. I recognize the man from the picture Jacob showed me a couple of weeks ago of the man he found lurking on Casey's property, pretending he was lost.

"Olivia." The man says my name and knocks on the window, but he doesn't knock with his hand. No, it's with the butt of the black gun in his hand that I didn't even see before now. "I need to have a word with you." My heart speeds up, but my feet stay stuck to the floor, and my stomach roils. "Just open the door and I promise I won't hurt you."

"Olivia!" I can still hear Casey yelling my name through my phone. I want to reach down and grab the phone, but the screaming in my head takes over, so I turn and run down the hallway. As I'm making my way up the stairs, the sound of glass breaking echoes in the silent house. My breathing now sounds like it's on speaker as I run to the end of the hall.

"Olivia." He says my name, and a shiver runs up my spine when I run toward the media room where Casey showed me a hidden closet. The sound of my heart thumping in my chest is the only thing I can hear as I turn to look over my shoulder. Seeing no one there, I go to the little closet that I laughed about when Casey showed me.

3

"What can you possibly keep in here?" I laughed, and then he knocked me on my ass with his answer.

"It's a hiding spot for my nieces and nephews," he said with a smile.

I open the closet door and climb in, closing it gently behind me so as not to make any noise. The sound of my heart pounding and my heavy breathing fills the small, dark space. I sit with my legs tucked to my chest in the darkness as my eyes get used to the darkness. The only light I see comes from the crack under the door.

"Olivia, don't make this any harder than it has to be," he says, and I close my eyes, hoping that this is a dream. But then I open my eyes again, and I'm still in the darkness. "Olivia." He says my name again, and this time, I hear the floor creaking under his feet as he makes his way farther into the house. "If you make me find you, it'll just be worse."

I try to swallow, but my throat is closed off, and only then do I realize tears are running down my face. My hands shake as I put them around my knees, and I think about how this is going to end.

How I'm going to die in this closet, and I haven't ever really fallen in love. I haven't even learned how to make my favorite meal yet. I haven't been to Bora Bora and swam in the blue water. I haven't ever had a man tell me he loves me and believe it. I've never been cherished. The tears now pour out like a river going downstream, and even if I tried to stop them, I don't think I would be able to. My body starts to shake, and I can hear my teeth chattering, and in the tight space, it sounds like it's full blast on speaker.

The sound of his footsteps makes my heart stop, and I hold my breath. "Olivia, just give me what I want, and I'll be gone."

I don't even know what he wants. I don't know what

anyone wants from me because I have nothing. I know nothing, yet every single day, I get two calls from blocked numbers.

"Don't make me angry," he says. His voice is getting louder, and I hear the creaking of the stairs as he climbs them.

"I have all the time in the world."

My breaths quicken, and my whole body shakes when I hear his footsteps coming closer. "I've been watching you," he says, and he sounds like he is right outside the closet door. Then I see a shadow under the door. I know he's close, so I hold my breath, hoping he doesn't find me and walks away. But instead, the sound of creaking fills the room, and I suck in a breath when he opens the door and stands there with a gun pointed at my face. "Hello, Olivia." He smirks, and a shiver runs up my spine. I take a second to look at the man who is going to end my life. For what, I will never know.

"Put down the gun." I hear Casey's voice, and I gasp when the man sneers at me, then turns around and shots are fired. I don't know what happens next because everything around me goes black.

Two

CASEY

"Olivia!" After screaming her name in the phone again, I strain to listen to what is going on when I hear a man's voice.

"Olivia," he says. My blood runs cold, and rage fills me from the tips of my toes to the top of my head. A rage I've never, ever felt before competes with the helplessness of not being there. I look at the phone, and my stomach sinks when I know I have to hang up and call Derek, my second in command at the security firm.

When I dial his number, it feels like forever before he answers even though it's less than one ring. "There is someone in my house!" I shout to him. "Get the feeds," I say and hang up before he can answer. Taking the curve to the farm faster than I should, I almost skid off the road with the rocks under the back tires.

I call Jacob next. He's the sheriff of the town and knows about Olivia and her situation. When it goes straight to voice mail, I take the phone in my hand and punch the steering wheel. I knew I shouldn't have left this morning. Something was telling me not to go. I should have listened to my gut, should have known it was too quiet and that things would all fall apart.

Twelve years ago, if you told me that I would end up owning almost half of my town, I would have laughed at you and called you crazy. I was a cowboy on the rodeo circuit making a name for myself. I wanted to take all the titles as rodeo king and then go home and raise my horses.

Well, my family's horses. Those were my goals and what I wanted to do. I mean, that and get married to my Lorelei and have a whole house full of kids. I was content in doing this because it was the only thing I knew.

Family tradition was to take over the family's mustang farm. But with just one word, one sentence, one heartbreak, the course of your life can change in a blink of an eye.

I played Russian roulette with my rodeo career, took a bet on myself, and I hung up my chaps.

Turning on the computer, I applied for community college. Who knew me playing on the computer in my first class would lead to me getting a contract with the military, which would lead to me opening one of the biggest security firms in the world. I now have fifteen international offices, and it's just growing. But I keep that life separate from Casey the farmer. The truth be told, the only people who really know are my family and Derek.

But my love is the farm where it first started, and it's where I learned how to be the man I am. Seeing the farm passed down from one generation to the next, I waited for my turn. Except I did it differently. I think back to when I got the farm and how I forced my father to sell it to me instead of handing it over.

When Kallie said she was coming back home, I thought it was strange, but after being away for eight years, it was a welcomed surprise. But then she arrived with her roommate, Olivia, who was running from something. Seems Olivia's ex-fiancé was caught with his hand in so many cookie jars it's surprising he still has both hands. He was arrested for embezzling, and her problems just got bigger and bigger. They thought she was in on it, and when someone leaked her name to the press, they pushed her into hiding. Kallie thought the farm would be the perfect place to get away, and I would have to agree with her.

But instead of just hiding out, she found that someone was after her. We had a picture of him, but we still didn't know anything about him or his motives. We knew nothing, and it just made this so much worse because it seemed we were chasing a ghost. We had to separate Kallie and Olivia, so it was a no-brainer that she would move in with me. I didn't think anything of it, but now having her in my house makes me smile. The little things she does to put a smile on my face. Like opening a beer as soon as I come home at around three or putting notes on the fridge about making today count. I always shake my head, but every day, I look for that note.

Forget that I want to have her naked under me. Forget that she is the most untouchable person I've ever met. I'm about to forget that I made a promise to myself to respect what she is going through and not push myself on her. But it was getting harder every single minute, especially with her in her shorts at night and her long legs. The only thing I could think of was having them wrapped around my waist.

I shake my head, directing my focus back to the road, but no matter how fast I drive home, it still seems as if it's farther and farther away. I dial my father, and I don't even let him say hello before I blurt out, "There is someone in my house."

"I'm ten minutes out," he says, and I hear him rushing around.

"I'll be there in two." Hanging up, I hold the phone in my hand like a lifeline to her when it rings, showing me it's Derek.

"Tell me something good," I hiss out when I answer him.

"Okay, he's going upstairs," he tells me, "but..."

"But what?" I shout at him when his voice trails off. "But what?" I repeat again.

"I can't find Olivia anywhere," he says, and I stop the car in front of my house. I lean over and open the glove box, taking out the gun I have in there. Making sure the safety is off, I listen to Derek talk. "I am going over the feed from before, but I haven't found her yet."

"Call Jacob. Tell him someone is on my property, and I'm going in loaded." Grabbing the handle, I'm pulling the door open when he says the next sentence, and I almost roar out.

"He's upstairs in the bedroom on the left," Derek says. "He's loaded with a Glock."

I leap up the steps of the front porch and enter the house as quietly as I can. Walking over to the stairs, I look up to see if the coast is clear. I walk up the first step and then turn to put my back to the wall as I climb the stairs with my gun in my hand locked and ready. My eyes never leaving the entrance to the media room, my eyes on the hallway, and then I hear him talking. "I've been watching you," he says. Now I know it's the guy who Jacob found on my property a couple of weeks ago. He's been lurking around but hasn't been caught. We haven't gotten anything on him, and trust me, we've been looking. My heart speeds up so fast as I try not to make any noise. Hoping like fuck the floors don't creak while I walk on them. I make it to the top of the stairs and tiptoe down the hall when I hear him say her name. "Hello, Olivia." A drop of sweat runs down my back, and I make it to the doorway. He stands there with his back to me, wearing black jeans and a black T-shirt. His black hair pulled back, his right arm outstretched as he points a gun at Olivia, and I make the mistake of looking at her. Tears are running down her beautiful face, her lips tremble, and her whole body shakes with fear.

A black rage rushes through me. *I'm going to make him*

pay, I think to myself, so I get into position, holding up my arms and making sure I aim. "Put down the gun," I say so calm even I wouldn't be scared of me. He turns around ever so slowly, and I know it's going to be either him or me.

It happens in slow motion. He turns around, his right arm outstretched, and when he faces me, I see the sneer on his face. Before I even realize it, shots are fired, and one of us goes down.

Three

OLIVIA

It happens in slow motion. The man with the gun pointed at my face sneers when he hears Casey's voice, and I want to yell for Casey to run away and let it be. But the words are stuck in my throat, and when the man turns around, I get one more glance of Casey. I think to myself he has to be the most beautiful man I've ever met, and I am thankful for having my time with him. Our eyes meet for one second before the sound of gunfire fills the room. Suddenly, all I feel is pain in my head, and I fade to black. I want to open my eyes and make sure Casey is okay, but the heaviness in them keeps them closed. My whole body feels so heavy I can't even lift my arm.

Casey sounds like he's right beside me as I float away. "Olivia!" He yells my name, and then I hear more noise, almost like a stampede of people coming up the stairs while I fade off. I think back to how this all started.

Watching the red elevator numbers go up one floor at a time, I felt my heart pounding in my chest. The brown box in my hand got heavier and heavier as the numbers got higher and higher. You can do this, *I told myself, cheering myself on. It's going to be fine. You need to just dump the box and go.*

The elevator pinged, and it took me back to two weeks ago when I walked down this exact brown plush rug toward Dominic's penthouse.

I tightened the strap on the trench coat that I was wearing over garters and a bra. My brand new Louboutins sank into the rug and pinched my feet as I licked my lips. Dominic had been gone all week, and he had just gotten back into town. He said he had a business meeting all night long with Chinese investors, but there I was, going to sneak into his penthouse and surprise him when he got back.

My key slid into the lock, and I pushed open the door, expecting the penthouse to be pitch black and quiet. Except it wasn't. The lights were on, and the whole open-floor concept was bright. From the doorway, I saw the empty living room, and the five open bottles of champagne on the kitchen island with five glasses. I walked to the counter, then heard the soft music coming from the bedroom. I knew I shouldn't go down there. I knew in my head it wasn't a good idea. Fuck, my brain was even telling me to turn around and walk out, pretending I didn't see anything, but my feet, those bitches had a mind of their own. I was halfway down the hall when I heard moaning, and my stomach flipped, nausea suddenly running through me. "So good." I heard a soft moan, and I knew that I was going to be heartbroken. Standing in the doorway of the master suite, I finally saw with my own eyes what my fiancé was up to. And if my feet didn't feel like they were glued to the floor, I would have stumbled back at the sight. Dominic had four women on the bed that we shared, the bed I slept in half the time.

He leaned over, snorting cocaine off a woman's stomach, then moved over to a second woman to do another line. The other two ladies were straddling the women's faces. He crawled over to one, grabbing her hair and pulling it back, then devoured her mouth, making her grind her hips even more. His cock was hard as a rock, and I had to wonder if he had taken anything since

*sex between us was usually a pitiful twenty minutes at best.
"Who's going to ride the cock first?"*

*"Me," the girl with the only mouth free said. "Last time, I
was last, so this time, I go first."*

*"Last time?" I whispered, but my voice was a bit too loud
because the girl who just spoke looked at me. She didn't move or
try to cover herself, though. Dominic, on the other hand, whipped
his head to the door, his eyes going wide as he saw me standing
there.*

*"What are you doing here?" he asked, all flustered as he got
off the bed. "You weren't supposed to be here."*

*"I'm sorry," I said to him. "I didn't mean to interrupt your
orgy!" I yelled at him. He walked toward me, but I held up my
hand. "Please don't come any closer to me."*

*"I can explain," he said, and I laughed. Looking over at the
bed, I saw that all the women were sitting in the middle of the
bed just watching.*

*"I think it's pretty self-explanatory as to what is going on
here. I don't need you to explain it as well." I pointed at the
women and saw the drugs on the side table next to our engagement picture. The one he had taken when he got down on one
knee in Hawaii in the middle of the beach with candles in the
shape of a heart and rose petals.*

"I have needs, Olivia," he said. "And I was very stressed."

*"Oh," I scoffed, "you look really stressed." I turned to walk
toward the door. "You looked so fucking stressed when you did
those two lines of cocaine off those girls." I shook my head. How
the fuck didn't I know he used cocaine? How the fuck was this
right under my nose, and I never knew it? I'd been around this
shit my whole life, so I knew all the signs. All of them.*

*"You can't just leave!" he shouted when I got to the door. I
turned around to face him as he stood there naked, and I looked
at him. He wasn't that attractive, if I was honest about it. His*

balding head showed that he'd had hair plugs. His nose had obviously been fixed. His teeth were all capped.

His body was mediocre, he rocked the dad bod like no one else I knew, and if I finally admitted it to myself, I was with him because he made me feel safe. He took care of me like no one else and made sure I was always okay. He put me first, and I put my head back. "We should discuss this."

"How long?" I asked him the only question I really cared about. "How long were you faithful?"

"Olivia," he said. "Baby face." He called me by the stupid nickname I hated, making me cringe, but then the anger of what I just walked in on took over me. The little piece of sanity I had come undone.

"How fucking long?" I shouted at the top of my lungs. "How fucking long have you been fucking other people?" I waited for it, just standing there. He was naked, and he just ... I loathed him. But that was what I was going to end up with. It was what I was going to end up with all along, and to me, it was what I deserved.

"That is not the point," he said, and I shook my head and laughed out bitterly.

"We've had unprotected sex!" I shouted. "So I think the point is, how fucking long, Dominic?" And then it all clicked into place. The all-night meetings he used to have. "Jesus." I laughed again. "I was so blind."

"If it means anything..." He looked down. "They don't mean anything."

Putting my hand to my chest, I said sarcastically. "That means so much." I turned around, opening the door. "Goodbye, Dominic."

I walked down the hallway and waited for him to follow me, but he didn't. I didn't know why that hurt more than walking in on him, but it did. That night, I went back to my apartment, and I told Kallie it was over.

She took one look at me and walked to the freezer, grabbing the full-fat ice cream and two spoons. "What are we watching?" she asked, and I put my head on her shoulder and ate ice cream.

"We need to take her in." I hear now, a groan comes out of me or at least I think I groan. I'm not even sure anymore. When I'm brought back down again into the blackness and the fog.

The door was busted open, pieces of wood flying all over the place. I didn't even know what was going on, but a gun was suddenly placed beside my temple while people were yelling all around me. "Get fucking down!" the guy yelled from right beside me. I didn't know what to do, I wasn't given a choice when he shoved me down to the floor. "I said on the fucking ground," he said again, his gun didn't move from the side of my head. This had to be a nightmare, I thought to myself as I was shoved down, the man got on top of me. His gun moved away from my temple, but the feeling was still there. "Hands behind your back." He pulled my hands behind my back, and the cold steel handcuffs were placed on me, and just like that, my life would never be the same.

"You need to let us help her." I feel hands on me, and I want to yell out not to touch me. I want to hide in a corner and make sure no one touches me, but I can't do anything. I can't move anything. My head burns, and right when I think I'm going to open my eyes, I fade off again.

Four

CASEY

With my gun drawn, I aim for his right shoulder and shoot as soon as he turns around. Before the guy knows what's happening, he stumbles back, and the gun falls from his hand. I watch as he advances closer, blood running down his arm, and the sound of him yelling fills the room. Reaching for the loose gun beside him, I keep my gun aimed on him, and I spot Olivia behind him. She's falling to the side, her head hitting the floor with the biggest bang I've ever heard. Her name rips through me. "Olivia!"

The front door opens. "Casey!" My father is yelling my name.

"Up here!" I say, looking down at the guy who has caused all this havoc. He rolls to the side with his left hand over his shoulder, blood leaking through his fingers. He looks like he is going to try something, so I make sure he knows I won't think twice about ending his life.

"Don't think I won't put one between your eyes," I hiss at him while he glares. The front door is smashed open again, and this time, it's more than one person as I hear the boots on the stairs. Looking over my shoulder, I see my father holding his own shotgun as he takes in the scene, and fear rushes through him as he scans the man on the floor.

"I'm good." He nods at me but doesn't put his gun down when he walks in.

Jacob's behind Dad with his gun drawn, wearing his bulletproof vest. Right behind him is Grady, his second in command. "Holy shit." He looks over at Grady, who nods at him when he puts his gun down and talks into the radio on his shoulder. "We need medics over at Casey's."

"Roger that." I hear as Grady walks over to the man who I refuse to let out of my sight. Even though my head is intent on getting to Olivia, my gun doesn't move.

"Do you have him?" I ask Grady. When he nods, I rush over to Olivia, who is slumped over.

"Olivia." I say her name softly while I take her in my arms. I hear her moan, but her eyes don't open.

"Is she hit?" my father asks, bending down next to me. I look over at him, he just looks into my eyes, his own eyes filling with tears. I ignore the burn creeping into my eyes as I hold her in my arms.

"I don't think so." I look for blood on her body, but there is none. But when I feel her head, I find a huge bump in the back. "She's got an egg-shaped bump on the back of her head," I say, holding her in my arms as close to me as I can, feeling her heat rush through me. "Olivia, darlin'." I say her name softly when I hear people coming up the stairs again. Two paramedics rush in, holding their medical bag.

"We have a gunshot wound on him," Grady says, pointing at the asshole in front of him. "And an unconscious woman." He points at Olivia, who is still in my arms.

One paramedic goes to the man, who is now sitting up with his hands cuffed behind his back. "You might have to take the cuffs off him."

He looks at Grady, who just shakes his head. "I checked

him before you guys got here. The bullet went right through, so you can cut the shirt off him."

"That's inhumane," the man whines, and if I didn't have Olivia in my arms right now, I would show him how inhumane I can be. My hands start to shake with anger and rage.

"Relax, son," my father whispers from beside me, and I look at him. We share a look, and he nods. The second paramedic comes over.

"What do we have?" he asks, and I look at him.

"I think she hit her head, but I'm not sure." I look back down at her, pushing her hair away from her face.

"You're going to have to lay her down so I can check her out," he says to me. I just look at him and then at Olivia in my arms. "I won't hurt her. But I can't do anything to help her if you don't let me." I place her down gently, hoping that she wakes up, but she doesn't. She just lies there limp. When I hear more footsteps on the stairs, I look up at the ceiling. Kallie appears in the doorway with tears in her eyes when she sees Olivia lying there.

"Olivia," she says, putting her hand to her mouth. The two of them have been best friends for a while, and they work together. She's about to take a step into the room when Jacob stops her.

"Kallie," Jacob says to her. "You shouldn't be here. It's a crime scene." She glares at him. The two of them have loved each other for a long time, but eight years ago, she ran away after he got one of his best friends pregnant. She left town the day after she found out and has not been back nor has she spoken to him since then.

She finally came back to town with Olivia. Everyone knows how hard it was for them to be face-to-face again. They have worked so hard to get back together, and I just hope that this time it sticks.

"This is my brother's property," she says. Turning to look at me, she hesitates to come into the big media room. "Mom is fit to be tied."

"I'll go to her," my father says, getting up and looking at me. He puts his hand on my shoulder, squeezing it. "She's going to be okay, son," he tells me, and I have nothing to say. I think I'm numb. I know I'm numb. I don't move from Olivia's side while the paramedic takes her vitals.

"We need to take her in," he says when Kallie kneels beside me. Her hand reaches out to touch Olivia's.

"Let's get him up," the other paramedic says. Grady leans down and pulls him up by his arm, making the guy wince. I watch him walk out of the room, not saying anything. My eyes stay fixated on the blood stain on the throw rug. I make a mental note to get it cleaned before Olivia comes home. Home. Is this even her home? This is only temporary, I know this. She is here only until it's safe for her to go home.

"We are going to transport her via ambulance to the hospital. The other victim will be going with Jacob."

"Victim?" I repeat the word. "He isn't a victim," I hiss, and Kallie puts her hand on my arm.

"Casey," she says, "let them take care of her."

"I can carry her out." I bend down, putting one hand under her legs and one under her back. She lies there in my arms with her head against my chest, and I shield her as I walk out of the room with her.

The whole time, I'm secretly begging her to open her eyes. I'm ready to do whatever needs to be done. "Darlin'," I whisper, "you need to open your eyes so I can see you." Holding her close to my chest, I say, "I just need to see your eyes." I walk toward the ambulance as the gurney waits for her. I shake my head, refusing to let her go. "I'm going with her."

"Okay, but it's best if we monitor her on the way to the

hospital," the paramedic says. "You can be right by her side." I nod as I place her gently on the gurney, still hoping she wakes up.

"Casey." I turn when I hear Jacob call my name. "We are going to follow you there. I have him in Grady's car," he says, and I look around for the first time. There are six cars in my driveway, all parked haphazardly with their police lights still on.

"If I see him ..." I look straight at Jacob.

"I know." He nods. I'm about to get into the ambulance when I hear my mother shout my name.

I look over at her, seeing her being held by my father. "Let me go, so help me God, Billy."

"Woman, you can't just run over there. This is police business," he tells her. I know that nothing he says will calm her, though. "Let him take care of Olivia."

"It's fine, Dad," I say, and she runs over to me. Her face is streaked with tears as she takes me in her arms and sobs. "I'm fine, Mom," I tell her, my eyes still on Olivia as they get her situated. "But I need to go."

"Okay." She releases me. "We'll meet you at the hospital."

"You don't have to," I say, and she just looks at me.

"Casey Christopher Barnes, don't you dare tell me what to do." I know I'm not going to win an argument when my mother uses my full name. It also doesn't help when she folds her arms over her chest because then you know she's waiting for a fight.

"I'll see you there." I lean down to kiss her on the cheek before turning to get into the ambulance. I watch as they take her blood pressure, but the whole time, she doesn't stir. "Is that normal?" I ask, sitting next to the paramedic. "I mean, for her to be out for so long?"

"It depends on how hard she hit her head. It could be a

number of things. But it could be that her body has gone into shock," he says, and I just nod, taking her hand in mine. Her soft, small hand with perfect fingers, the same fingers that I held when we walked out of the bar last week.

"You want to hold my hand, cowboy?" she said with a glimmer in her eye.

I didn't answer her then, but I would answer her now. I bring her hand to my mouth, whispering, "I want to hold your hand, darlin'," then kiss the tips of her fingers.

Ever since she came to town, I've wanted to touch her all the damn time, and I even kissed her a couple of times. Each time, it was harder and harder not to keep kissing her. I have been itching to do so again. I try not to touch her as often as I want, knowing that one touch will not be enough. But something about her just makes me do things that I know I shouldn't. Having her in my house and all around me means the little touches happen anyway. Even though I try not to think about it now. Feeling her hand in mine, I wonder why I haven't done it more.

"We are five minutes out," the driver says. When we get to the hospital, everything happens so fast, and I don't know where she's going. Two nurses and two doctors are waiting there for us, and they take her out so fast, I have to run after them. When they rush past two swinging doors, one of the nurses stops me from entering.

"You need to stay here, and I'll come out as soon as I know something," she says, and I'm about to walk past her. "I know you want to get in there, but all you'll do is get in the way. She is in the best hands right now, so let them do their job. I promise you that I will let you know when we know something."

"She's been unconscious this whole time," I say. She nods, then turns to walk back through the doors. I look through the little glass window as she runs to the room where they have taken Olivia. I stand here, and my eyes don't move from the room where I know they are working on Olivia.

"Any news?" Kallie says from beside me, and my head just shakes. I don't even know how long she's been standing there.

"Nothing," I say, but my eyes don't move. "They said when they have an update, they'll find me and let me know."

"She's going to be fine." She puts her arm through mine. "She's the strongest woman I know." I don't agree with her; she's more than the strongest woman. She's the most thoughtful also. She does little things just to help, like making sure the coffee in the barn is started for me when I get there. She just has this energy, and you just want to sit with her and let her talk to you, or just sit with her on the swing and watch her watch nothing.

"Hey." Hearing Jacob, I turn to look at him, and then back again to make sure I didn't miss anything.

"Hey," Kallie says to him. She slips her arm out of mine, then goes over to Jacob and looks up at him. He leans down, kissing her on the lips. "Did you find out who the guy was?" she asks. I've been waiting to hear that answer.

I turn now, looking at Jacob who just looks at me. "We got his name, but he lawyered up the minute he got in the car. Grady found his car, and he was not a rookie, that's for sure." I can see there is more he wants to share, but he doesn't.

We don't say anything else as we wait at the doors, each of us in our own thoughts. I don't know how long we stay here, but when the doctor comes out of the room, he walks straight to the doors. He looks at Jacob, who nods at him, and then looks at me. "I think it's best if we talk in private."

He turns, walking into another room, then waits for all three of us to step in before closing the door. When I see Jacob take a sobbing Kallie in his arms, I realize this is the room where they take you when it's bad. With the two couches in the room, it's what's always described to you when the doctor tells you that your loved one is dead.

I stand here, not moving as my body turns to stone. I hold my breath as the doctor takes a seat and starts. "I'm sorry."

Five

OLIVIA

"We need to get her an MRI and see if there is swelling." The voice sounds far away, but I'm not sure where I am. I feel pressure on my arm, and my eye being forced opened. A light is shining in my eye, and I groan, or at least I think I do. My hand is lifted, and I feel something placed on my index finger. "Her body is going into shock," someone says, and then suddenly, darkness takes me back into my nightmare.

After being arrested, I was thrown into a cell for over four-teen hours. Fourteen hours of trying to get anyone to talk to me, fourteen hours of sobbing quietly, fourteen hours of sitting in a jail cell. A fucking jail cell. I had never even had a fucking parking ticket, and now I was now sitting in a fucking cell. They finally came to get me, ushering me into a room where two detectives were waiting for me.

The room had a rectangle table against the wall, one chair against the wall while two chairs sat facing the one. I sat in the chair facing the two detectives. "Olivia." The one guy leaned back in the chair. "I'm just going to cut right to the chase."

I didn't know if it was at that moment that I started to

shake, or maybe it was the fact that my body went into shock, but one of them got up, walking out of the room. "What am I doing here?" I asked through my chattering teeth. The other guy came back with a blanket and a bottle of water. The first thing I'd been given in fourteen hours.

"You really have no idea what is going on?" one of them asked, and I shook my head. I tried to put the blanket around me, but my hands were shaking so hard I couldn't even hold it.

"Your fiancé, Dominic Albano, was arrested for swindling over thirty million dollars from his clients in a Ponzi. That is just scratching the surface," he said.

I looked at them shocked, the back of my neck suddenly heated. "What?" I asked, looking at each of them. "I don't understand. Dominic works as an investment adviser." I told them exactly what he told me. "He also dabbles in the stock market."

They both chuckled. "Dabble? The man is a con artist." He shook his head. "How much did you know?"

I looked at them. "Nothing," I told them. "For all I know, he works with the stock market, and he is an independent investment adviser."

"He was your fiancé," one of them said.

"Ex," I told them. "Ex-fiancé, which is why I was at his house yesterday. I was returning his stuff." They shared a look, and then one looked down. "I had no idea what he was doing was illegal. Had I known, there was no way I would have actually stayed with him." They both looked at me with blank stares. "Look, I don't know what's going on here, but I do know this. I had no idea, not one that he was shady as fuck. I walked in on him having an orgy last week, so I was at his place to return his stuff." I put my shoulders back, looking straight ahead. "With that said, I want my lawyer. I have nothing to hide, but I'm not going to chance it by saying something I shouldn't." It took another ten hours to get me out after

Dominic admitted I had nothing to do with it. I walked out of jail, not expecting the media to be there camping out as they snapped pictures.

"The doctor said she can hear everything." I hear Kallie say sniffling, and I could swear she is crying. "So we have to keep it upbeat." Kallie is the best friend I've ever had. Actually, the only friend I've ever had who has ever had my back. Who would have thought that after agreeing to do a Christmas special at work, the two of us would get along so well? We work for the same magazine; she is a graphic designer while I am a fashion stylist. I basically tell her what I want, and she makes it happen. We clicked so well that we decided to become roommates.

"Kallie." I hear Jacob, and I want to laugh. I would kill to lift my hand or even wiggle my toes. I focus on wiggling my toes, expecting my feet to move. I groan in frustration when they don't, and the talking around me stops.

"Darlin'?" I hear Casey, then feel my hand picked up, and I groan again. He brings my hand to his lips, and I want to tease him about holding my hand. But instead, my head pounds; it's almost like there is a jackhammer in there. I groan again, and this time, my eyes flutter open. But I close them just as fast when the light is too bright.

"Too," I say in a whisper, licking my lips, "bright."

"Turn off the lights," Casey orders. "Jacob, get the shades."

I open my eyes again slowly, not knowing if I will be able to, but they flutter open again. It's better. "Hey there, darlin'." I look over at Casey, seeing the anguish in his eyes. I want to ask him if he's okay. I want to ask so much, but my mouth is so dry.

"Don't talk. Jacob went to get the nurse," Kallie says from beside me. I look over to see her face stained with tears. I'm about to ask her if anyone else is hurt, and I suddenly start to panic, thinking maybe the man hurt Charlotte or Billy before coming to me. But a nurse swings the door open.

"Well, well, that was quite a nap." She smiles, coming over to the side where Kallie is. "I know that one is not going to let go of your hand," she says, motioning with her head to Casey, who just glares at her, and she laughs. "So I'm going to take your vitals on this side." She takes my blood pressure. "How are you feeling?"

"Head hurts," I say, closing my eyes but not for long because I'm so scared I'll get sucked under again.

She takes off the armband, the sound of the Velcro making me wince. "Only normal. You got a big bump on your head."

Lifting my hand, I feel my head, finding the big bump on my head. "How?"

"I think when the shot fired, you got so scared you smacked your own head into the wall," Casey says, his voice soft, while my hand is still warm in his. He doesn't loosen his grip on me, and I don't move my hand away from his.

The door opens, and this time, the doctor enters with a smile. Then he looks over at Casey who glares at him. "I see we are calmer." I look from the doctor to Casey, wanting to ask what is going on, but the door opens again. Charlotte comes in, sobbing when she sees me with my eyes open. Her hands go to her mouth as she comes over to me and almost pushes Casey to the side.

"Oh my Lord," she says, taking my face into her hands. "You had us all worried," she says. "Can she eat?" she asks the doctor, and the doctor just looks at her.

"I've never seen an emergency room overtaken by family before," he says. I want to correct him and tell him that they aren't my family, but for this one time, I pretend I have a family who cares. A family who would go above and beyond for each other. "If you'll just give us five minutes to examine her, then she's all yours," he says. Kallie nods, turning to walk out, followed by Jacob, Charlotte, and Billy. "You are obviously going to stay?" he asks Casey, who just looks at him.

"Obviously," he says, and I look over at the nurse who is biting her lips to stop herself from laughing out loud. The doctor takes my vitals again, then looks at me.

"You have a concussion," he says. "Your body went into shock, which is why you were unconscious for so long." He puts his stethoscope around his neck, tucking his hands into the pockets of his white lab coat. "As I mentioned to you"—he looks at Casey—"after you let me speak ..." I look back at Casey, who just rolls his eyes. "I told you she would wake up when she was ready."

"I heard you," Casey says.

"If everything looks good, she can go home tonight. But," he says, and I look at him, "it's best if she gets rest and no television or computer."

"For how long?" I ask him, thinking of all the work that will pile up.

"At least seven days. After seven days, if you turn on the television or computer, and you get a headache, you have to turn it off and start over at day one again," he says. I don't even want to think about how I'm going to work if I can't use my computer. "If the headache is really bad, I want you to come in."

"I'll make sure she follows the rules," Casey says from beside me. The doctor just nods at him, then walks out of the room with the nurse.

"Cowboy," I say. He shakes his head but doesn't look at me. My heart sinks when he doesn't look at me. Why would he look at me when I've caused him all this headache? Why would he even want to talk to me after I brought this danger to his house? He could have been hurt; his family could have been hurt. I take a deep breath and wipe away the tear that falls with my hand. "I'm sorry," I whisper. He looks at me shocked, and before I tell him that I'm going to leave, the door opens and Charlotte comes in with a bag in her hand.

"I brought soup," she says, smiling. "In case you're hungry."

I slowly pull my hand away from Casey's even though it suddenly feels cold. "Thank you," I tell her. Kallie just stares at me as I try to get her to hear my thoughts without saying a word. "But I'm not hungry."

"She probably just needs to rest," Kallie says. I look down at my hands, trying not to face Billy and see his disappointment in me.

"We should go," Billy says. I try not to cry, but he comes close to the bed and leans down. "We'll see you at home," he says, softly kissing my cheek. I close my eyes, trying not to sob out.

Charlotte is the next one to me, and she doesn't go soft like Billy does. No instead, she sits on the bed next to me and pulls me to her. Her arms go around me, and I want nothing more than to sink into her hug. "I'm going to go home and prepare all your favorite foods," she says. I want to tell her not to, but if I say anything, the sob might rip through me.

"We'll walk you out," Jacob says, sharing a look with Casey. I don't look over at Casey because I'm afraid to see the disappointment on his face. "Casey," Jacob calls him, and I think he's going to fight him, but instead, he pushes away and gets up.

"I'll be back," he says softly, my eyes watching Kallie. She waits for the door to close before she turns and looks at me.

"What's the matter?" she asks. I try to look at her, but my tears cloud my vision.

"I need you to get me out of here," I say, and her mouth opens in shock. "It's not safe, and I refuse to put you or your family in anymore danger."

"You have to be insane," she hisses. "You must have hit

your head harder than I thought if you think I'm going to let you escape." She folds her arms over her chest.

"I can't do it," I say, and the sob finally rips free. "I can't see the disappointment in their eyes." Throwing the covers over my legs, I climb out of bed and turn to walk out. I must move too fast because my head spins, and the next thing I know, I'm on the floor, and Kallie is yelling for help as the blackness takes me again.

Six

CASEY

I don't want to leave her. I don't want to walk out of this room without her, but I can tell Jacob wants to tell me something that he doesn't want to share with Olivia.

"What's so urgent?" I ask him once we get outside the room.

Jacob glances at the door behind me. "He's gone," he says. My hand starts to shake, and Jacob sees it. "Relax." He shakes his head, then leans in close. "The feds came and took him."

"What?" I ask, confused. "Why?"

"Seemed he was working with a certain person in prison," he says. I don't know what to say. How can someone who loves someone or at least pretends to love someone want them to be harmed? "They got wind we had him, and it took them an hour to get here."

I look at him speechless. "So you want to discuss almost killing the doctor?" he asks. I glare at him, and I'm about to tell him to fuck off when I hear Kallie yell. Rushing back in the room, I see Kallie trying to pick up Olivia from the floor.

"What the fuck?" I almost push Kallie away harder than I want to. "Move," I tell her, crouching down to pick Olivia up

31

and put her back on the bed. "Darlin'," I whisper when she moans.

The nurse comes rushing in, and I turn to see that Kallie is crying in Jacob's arm. "What is all the commotion?" the nurse asks.

"She was ..." Kallie starts to say, then stops, and I know she's hiding something. "She was getting up, thinking she was okay to leave, and she fell."

"She fell?" I ask. Putting my hands on my hips, I look at her, then I look at the nurse. "Did she hit her head again?"

"No," Olivia mumbles, her eyes open. I don't know why I breathe a sigh of relief. *It's only because you have the need to take care of her since she lives in your house*, I tell myself, but the other part of me laughs. Lies. It's all lies. "I just got up too fast. I must have been lightheaded because my head started to spin, and I couldn't catch myself before I fell." She doesn't look at me, and if there weren't so many people in the room, and she didn't have a concussion, I would hold her face in my hands and force her to look at me.

"How about we get you something to eat?" the nurse says, so I do the only thing I can do. I stand here by her bed.

"My mother brought soup," I tell the nurse who nods. Kallie walks over to the bag my mother left. She takes out a soup bowl, then pours the soup out of the thermos.

"Just don't overdo it," the nurse says. "We'll check with you in a bit and see how you are feeling."

"I won't," Olivia says softly. The phone in my back pocket vibrates. I take it out to see that it's Derek.

"I'll be right back," I say, looking over at Jacob. "Stay with her until I get back." He just nods.

"Hello," I say into the phone. Walking out of the room, I stand with my back against the wall, facing the door. I make sure I have her in my sight through the small window in the door.

"Hey, how is she?" he asks. I look down, putting my hand behind my neck. My neck is starting to get sore from the tension that I now have every single time I walk away from her. The need to stay by her side to make sure she is okay is so strong I don't know how to fight it. It's bigger than me. I want to sit with her and hold her hand. I want to tuck her hair behind her ear. I want to whisper to her that everything is going to be okay. I want it all, but I know that she is only here temporarily, and that it's better for both of us not to go there.

"She has a concussion," I say. "What did you learn?" Derek and I met when we were paired together for a project two weeks into our computer class. The two of us were unstoppable, and when we aced the class, we continued to work together. If there is stuff out there to be found, Derek will find it. There is nothing that you can hide from him. It's why the government uses us; it's why we have what we have. I develop the programs, and he just makes them that much better.

"Phillip "the barber" Conserto." He whistles. "This guy has a rap sheet that started when he was twelve and was placed into foster care when his mother took off and his father died." I wait for the bad stuff. Knowing Derek, he starts off slow and then gives you all the important stuff at the end. "In and out of juvie until he was eighteen, and then did six months for intent to sell. Graduated to full-blown murder by the time he was twenty. The case was tossed out when he asked for a lawyer and they continued to question him, so his confession was not admissible and he only did two years. During that time, he made lots of friends in Rikers. The kind of friends who don't send you Christmas cards either. Got really close to Jake Biotti who was in there for money laundering but more importantly for killing someone and all kinds of shit that screams mob."

"Why do I need to know this?" I ask, and he laughs.

"Trust me, I would not be telling you this for no reason. He got out, and suddenly, the only witness to the case for murder was missing. Turns out, she still hasn't been found, but her parents get a letter every year with her hair. That's how he got his nickname "the barber." From then on, he became his own contractor. They have him associated with about seventy-two missing witnesses, but nothing sticks to him."

"Where is he going now?" I ask, looking into the room where Olivia puts down the spoon and leans back in the bed. *She is too pale*, I think to myself.

"I'm waiting for them to place him, and then I'll get eyes on him," he says. "According to what I can find out, it looks like he was hired by Dominic to get to Olivia. Dude, this guy has nothing but bad news written all over him."

"Jesus fuck, why the fuck would he want to take her out when she knows nothing?" I ask.

"I can't answer that," he says, "but I'm trying to find out."

"Let me know if anything changes, and I want only you working on this. I also want more eyes on my house. This guy literally walked up to my house, and nothing was triggered."

"He found the wires," Derek says. "There is a feed of him arriving today, finding the one wire, and snipping it."

"Well, you know what that means. We need to get some wires that are triggered when cut," I say, and I feel the headache coming on.

"On it," he says and disconnects. The door opens, and Jacob comes out.

"Everything okay?" he asks as I put my phone away.

"No," I answer him. "Nothing about this is okay. Something isn't adding up," I say. Olivia's door opens again, and Kallie steps out into the hallway.

"Did she eat?" I ask, and she nods.

"Just a bit, but then she threw up," she says. I'm about to charge into the room, but then she adds, "The nurse said it's

34

normal." I look into the room now and see she is turned on her side. Her eyes are closed again, and my heart speeds up, thinking that it's too soon for her to go to sleep. She should stay awake a little longer. I see the nurse writing something in her chart.

"Casey." Kallie draws my attention back to her. "You need to relax a bit."

"I am relaxed," I lie to her, and she just rolls her eyes. "Listen, she lives in my house. I just want to make sure she is okay. All this happened on my property, so it's my responsibility."

"Is that what you're telling yourself?" Kallie says, trying to hide the smile on her face. "We are going to go to the cafeteria and get some coffee. Do you want anything?"

"No," I say as I walk past them to enter the room. The nurse looks over at me and puts her finger to her lips.

"She was tired," she whispers. "Push the button if you need anything." She walks out quietly. I walk over to the bed where she's lying on her side. I sit in the chair watching her, and it finally dawns on me the danger that she was in. It finally dawns on me that she could have lost her life today. Everything that Derek told me makes this even more real. He would have killed her without a second thought. And then what? I would have gotten strands of her hair for the rest of my life. I watch her chest rise and fall, trying not to think of the look on her face when I walked into the media room. Seeing a gun pointed right at her face and all the fear that was etched on it. I try to block out how when she fell, my heart literally stopped beating. She moans, then her eyes flutter open, and she looks at me. "You okay?" I ask, leaning in.

"Yeah," she whispers and then looks away from me. "You don't have to stay here, Casey."

I try not to let her words cut me. Maybe she doesn't want me here. "I am not here because I have to be here." I lean in, putting my elbows on my knees. "I'm here because I want to be here."

I'm expecting her to fight me on this, but she doesn't. Instead, she just closes her eyes again. "I just want to go home." She takes a deep breath. "Just want it over with."

"As soon as the doctor gives you the okay, we'll get you home," I say. Reaching out, I take her hand in mine, and I don't care. The need to feel her heat run through me is something bigger than I can say or admit. "You know Mom is going to be cooking until the sun comes up."

She doesn't pull her hand away from me. "I'm sorry, Casey," she says again.

"Sorry for what, darlin'?" I ask. Leaning over the bed, I wipe away the tear rolling down the side of her face with my thumb. Her beautiful face, her blue beautiful eyes dark with worry and fear, instead of light with happiness.

"I'm sorry that I brought all this to your farm," she says. "I'm sorry that all of this is happening. I shouldn't have come here."

"None of this is your fault," I tell her, hoping she hears me. "Not one thing that happened today is your fault."

She shakes her head. "What if your mom was over?" she says with a sob. "What if your father got hurt instead of me?" She shakes her head. "What if he shot you?"

Her words echo in my head. "Were you the one holding the gun?" She looks at me. "Were you the one who broke into my house? No," I tell her, hoping she understands me. "None of this is your fault, so get that thought out of your head." I'm about to lean in to kiss her just to taste her and feel that she's okay, but the door opens and Kallie walks in.

"Guess what I found?" she says, smiling. "Tea."

Olivia moves her hand out of mine and turns to sit up. All I can do is sit here hoping that I'm still standing at the end of this.

Seven

OLIVIA

I want nothing more in the whole world than for this mess to go away so I can just be a normal fucking person. Just for once, I want to be the normal person who works, meets a man, and then falls in love. I want the white picket fence, and maybe, one day I'll get to be a mom.

I mean, it's not like I had any good role models growing up. My mother was ... well, she's a bitch. She lived through me my whole life. Almost like I was a show monkey that she would parade beside. I shake my head when the tears pinch my nose. The door opens, and the nurse comes in. "Well, don't you look better."

"I feel okay," I tell her. I hear Casey exhale a huge breath beside me, but I don't look at him. I can't look at him. I'm afraid the minute I look at him, I'm going to sob like a baby and ask him to hold me. Since I've been here, he has given me more hugs than I can count. I feel safe in his arms and know that no matter what happens, I will be okay. He doesn't give those fake side hugs like everyone else I know. Nope, not with Casey. I've been on the runway more times than I care to admit with models who have chiseled faces and perfect bodies, yet this man with a little stubble on his face, his piercing blue eyes, and dirty blond hair ... he's what perfect is.

"Well, it looks like you can go home," she says. I almost clap my hands, but I'm afraid my head would throb. "How is the head?"

"I have a headache." I'm honest with her. "At least ... it feels like a headache."

"That's normal," she says, and I smile at her. "If it gets worse, or you have trouble keeping your eyes open, you need to come back. Now I need to know that you will have someone with you to help you."

I'm about to tell her that I'm leaving as soon as I get to Casey's house and pack my stuff. I'll go stay in a hotel and hire a nurse if I have to. "She's with me. I'll check on her."

The nurse smiles at me and then turns to Casey. "She should be woken up every two hours. Just make sure she is coherent and stays hydrated."

He gives the nurse the smirk that I'm sure makes all the girls go crazy. "I can do that." She walks past him out of the room.

Kallie looks at me, then looks at Casey. "Why don't you go get the truck?" She hands him the keys and pushes him out.

"Make sure she uses a wheelchair," he says right before she closes the door on him, shaking her head. But he just knocks, and I have to laugh when I look over and see his face pressed to the little window. "Wheelchair," he says. Kallie sticks up her middle finger at him. He looks at me, smiling, and just like that, he's gone.

"Okay, missy," she says, coming over to the bed and sitting down beside me. "I need you to promise me that you aren't going to sneak out of the house in the middle of the night." I look down at my hands.

"I'm not kidding." When her voice goes low, I look over at her, and she has tears running down her face. She's been my best friend and as close to a sister as I have ever had. I would do anything for her, and I know she would do anything for me, which is why we're back in the town she ran away from eight years ago.

"Olivia." When she presses for an answer, I swear all my words are stuck in my throat. Knowing she put aside her heartache to come back to this town for me is everything, and I could never repay her for it.

She takes my hand in hers. "You know, if we don't get out of here, Casey is probably going to drive the truck in here."

I nod at her, getting up, slipping off the hospital gown that they made me change into when I threw up to put my clothes back on. "I don't think I could ever repay you."

"What are you talking about now?" Kallie looks at me.

"For all this. I don't ..." The sob comes out, and she comes over to me, holding my face in her hands.

"If it wasn't for you, I wouldn't have the love of my life back," she says. "If it wasn't for you, I would still be existing and not living life." She wipes my tears away with her thumbs, just like her brother did not too long ago. "I should be the one thanking you."

She's about to say something else when my phone rings in her pocket, and after she looks at the screen, she shows me it's Casey. Putting it on speaker, she doesn't even have time to say anything before he barks out, "What's taking you so long? Is she okay? Does she want me to come in and carry her out?" I smile at the sound of his voice. I have no choice.

"Relax there, cowboy. I'm changing my clothes. We'll be right out," I say. Taking the phone from her, I hang up on him when he starts issuing orders about the nurse and the wheel-chair. "Is he always like this?" I ask, and she shakes her head.

"Never," she says, and I'm afraid to ask her what she means. The door opens and the nurse comes in with the wheelchair. "We just got a call at the nurses' desk about you needing a wheelchair." She tries to hide her smile, pretending she's annoyed, but I can see it written all over her face. She is another one who has fallen for Casey's charms.

I roll my eyes and shake my head as I go take a seat in the chair. She wheels me out, and I see him leaning against the truck with one foot up. He's wearing blue Levi's with his white T-shirt. He looks to the side, and I have a second where I watch him. He must sense that I'm watching him because he turns and looks at me, his whole face lights up with a smile.

"There you are," he says with his Southern accent, making my stomach flip. He holds out a hand for me, and I take it, expecting him to hold my hand while I get in the truck, but instead, he picks me up like a baby and places me in the front seat. I'm so shocked I have nothing to say while he buckles me in and then closes the door. Walking over to the nurse, he kisses her on the cheek, making her blush. "Now you bring your granddaughter over to the farm, and we'll get her riding some horses."

"Will do," she says, turning to walk back into the hospital with the empty wheelchair. Kallie gets into the truck.

"He's lost his mind," I say as she fastens her seat belt. I watch him walk around the truck and get in.

"Shall we go home?" he asks. I want to tell him that my home is in Los Angeles, but I just nod. I look out the window into the dark night as he makes his way home. When we pull up to his house, all the lights are on, and his parents are sitting on the porch waiting for us.

"What a shocker," Kallie says from the back and gets out of the truck. I reach for the handle, but the door is being opened by Billy.

"Hey there, pretty girl." He puts out his hand to help me down, and I take it. I don't know what to do with all these people around me trying to help. I've never had this before.

He holds my hand, walking with me to the porch where

Charlotte stands with tears in her eyes. "I was so worried," she says, taking me in her arms, and I hug her with the one hand I have available. "Are you hungry?" she asks me.

"I think I just want a hot shower," I say. I would actually kill for a bath, but I'm not going to ask Casey to sit in his bathtub. Billy releases my hand, and I walk into the house with Charlotte, her arm around my shoulder. She takes me straight to my bedroom, and I see that the bed has been turned down.

"I didn't know if you were hungry or not, so I just left you some water and a couple of muffins by your bed." She points at the huge basket of muffins and the two water bottles beside my bed. "In case you are too tired to get out of bed."

"Thank you so much," I say, smiling at her. Walking over to the bed, I sit down, not admitting that it took way more energy than I have just to walk into the house. Over the years, she has come to visit maybe once or twice. I knew right away that she was the mom I wanted to be when my time came, whenever it did. A mother who puts her kids first, a mother who nurtures and loves unconditionally. Not just because you won first prize or were selected to walk in the Victoria's Secret fashion show.

"You didn't have to do that." She wrings her hands in front of her, looking like she wants to say something, so I take all my remaining strength to get up and go over to her.

"Are you okay?" She looks at me, and she has tears in her eyes.

"I'm just ..." I want to tell her that I'm sorry that I brought all this to her. "I was so scared that you were going to be hurt." She blinks, but a tear falls anyway. "But now I see for my own eyes you're okay."

My own tears gather in my eyes when I look at her; this woman, who is as simple as can be, and all she wants is to have her daughter home. My mother, on the other hand, has everything that she can buy at her fingertips, and the last thing she wants is for me to come home.

"Oh, Charlotte," I say, hugging her. "Thank you for having me, and I'm so, so sorry," I finally say out loud. "I'm going to make a couple of phone calls tomorrow. I'll find somewhere else to go."

She looks at me in shock. "You will do no such thing," she says. "When you finally get settled, we'll have a family meeting to discuss whatever is going on. But whatever it is, we handle it here."

"But I'm not family," I say, trying not to let the sting hurt so much.

She puts her hand on mine. "Oh, hush your mouth, silly girl." She smiles through the tears. "You're one of us now." I don't answer her. Instead, I blink away the tears that are stinging my eyes, and all I hear is my mother's voice.

"Tears are a waste, Olivia. No one is going to want such a dramatic woman."

"Thank you," I say, and she gets up.

"You go take a shower. I'll send Casey to check on you later." She walks out of the room.

Walking over to the drawer, I open it to grab my stuff, then walk into the bathroom. I turn on the lights, but they're too bright, so I turn them off and make my way through the dark to the shower. With just the little light shining into the bathroom from the room, I undress and step under the hot water. And as it pours over my face, I let the tears fall.

I sob, wondering how I got myself into this mess. I should have walked away long before Dominic proposed. I shouldn't have settled, but all I could hear is my mother's voice.

"Olivia, you never marry for love. You marry for money; the bigger the wallet, the bigger the happiness. You marry a man who has a private plane, not one who cleans them."

I didn't even love him. I tolerated him. I mean, in the

beginning, he treated me like a princess. He took me on these romantic little dates, but then the dates got less romantic and more extravagant. So I would forget the small stuff, like how he sent me flowers every time we went out the first month, and then they just stopped. God, I was so stupid, and now look at where I am. In the middle of the South trying to make sure the people I love don't get hurt.

When I get out, it takes everything in me to dry off and put my pjs on. When I open the door, the only light in the room is coming from the little lamp on the nightstand. I walk over to the bed and slide into it. I should tell them I'm okay, but the minute my head hits the pillow, I'm sucked into sleep.

The darkness takes over, and I'm suddenly standing in the middle of my apartment. Except it's vandalized exactly like it was in the pictures that they showed me a couple of weeks ago. I look around and see that our couches are shredded like people thought we were hiding something in them. The stuffing is scattered around it, and the coffee table is tossed over on its side. I look over at the shattered television. Walking over to the kitchen, I see that all the cabinets are open, everything is thrown on the floor, and the fridge is tipped over. When I turn to walk to my bedroom, I stand in the doorway, seeing my stuff on the floor and smashed to bits. The pictures I had on the wall are thrown on the floor, and the walls have holes in them. My bed is flipped over, and the mattress is cut right down the middle. My drawers are all over the floor, and my clothes or whatever is left are scattered. And I can't forget the red writing on my bedroom wall.

You'll get what's owed to you.

I hold up my hand to the wall, my fingers reaching out to touch it, but I'm suddenly in Casey's house. I'm standing in the living room, and the writing is on his wall. His whole house is trashed, as I stand in the middle of it. The front door opens, and when I look over, Dominic comes in, looking at me. "You can't outrun me this time." He raises his hand and aims a gun at me and then shoots. The sound of yelling makes my eyes fly open when I realize I'm the one screaming.

Casey runs into the room, and he has me in his arms before I can take my next breath. I'm gasping for breath and trying to get my heart to slow, but all I can do is sob and cling to Casey while he holds me.

Eight

CASEY

The sound of her screaming makes my blood run cold. Jumping off the couch, I run over to her room and find her thrashing in her bed. "It's okay," I say. Her eyes open with a wild look in them. "I got ya, darlin'." I hold her in my arms as she sobs, clinging to me, then I climb into bed next to her when she finally calms down. "Do you want something to drink?" She just shakes her head but doesn't move from my arms.

"Can we go lie on the couch?" she asks, her voice weak. Standing, I gather her in my arms and carry her to the couch. "Why is there a pillow and blankets already here?" she asks when I put her down so her head is on the pillow. Sitting next to her on the couch, I cover her with the same blanket I was using.

"Well, I was afraid I wouldn't hear you if something happened," I say as I push the hair away from her face. "I promised my mother that I would take care of you." The lie comes out before I can stop it. My mother had no say in where I slept. She left the house as soon as she came out of the room. I just wanted her gone so I could be alone with Olivia. I listened at her door, and when I didn't hear anything, I walked in and turned off the overhead light, then switched on the small lamp on the nightstand. Situating myself outside her room, I sat with my back to the wall, and waited until she came out and climbed into bed. Once I heard her soft snores, I went to my bathroom and took the fastest shower of my life. After I finished, I checked on her again, then decided to sleep on the couch since I'd have to set my phone alarm for two hours to remember to wake her. It rang quietly once, but my eyes were still open. I got up and walked over to her. Checking on her, I felt like a creep watching her, but I just stared at her, wondering what in the fuck was going on with me. Until I heard her yelling.

She swallows while she looks at me, and I walk to the fridge to get her a bottle of water.

"Here," I tell her as I open, then hand her the bottle. I walk to sit down on the couch beside her feet. She swallows a couple of sips. "How is your head?"

Looking down at her hands, she says, "It almost feels like I have a little headache." She takes another sip, and I wait a couple of minutes.

"You feeling any better?"

She nods. "Yeah, it was a nightmare." When her head shakes, a tear escapes, but she wipes it away.

"It's only normal, darlin'," I tell her softly. "Yesterday was crazy."

"It was a weird one," she says, looking at me. "I was standing in my apartment, but it was trashed, and then suddenly, I was standing in this room. But it was trashed, too." She leans over to set the water bottle on the coffee table. "It's fine. It was just a dream."

"It was," I say softly, wanting to cup her cheeks with my hands. I want to sleep with her in my arms so she can feel protected and safe.

"Is it okay if I sleep here on the couch?"

I want to tell her that she should sleep in my bed, but I don't want her to think that I want anything. So instead, I just nod. "Sure, darlin'." She turns to her side and closes her eyes.

"Thank you, Casey," she says softly, and I don't answer her because I don't trust the words that would come out of my mouth. Instead, I get up and walk back to my bedroom to grab another pillow. When I walk back out, she's already snoring softly.

When I decided to build this house, I knew my vision. I built it from the ground up with my own hands. I did have help, but I poured my blood, sweat, and tears into this house to make it exactly like I wanted. It was the same as my parents' but with a modern touch. The family room, unlike my parents' house, has high ceilings, and when you turn, you can see the railing to the second floor. The couch we are sitting on was custom made. I wanted a huge U-shaped one with huge pillows to face the fireplace with a big-screen television over it. Even though I barely watch television, I bought a ninety inch.

I'm about to put my pillow on the other end of the couch when Olivia whimpers in her sleep. I stop and turn. Walking back over to her, I look down at her, and the whimpers stop. She rolls over to face the other way, and when I turn to walk to my side, she whimpers again. *Walk away, Casey*, I tell myself. Nothing good is going to come from this. Just walk away. But when she whimpers again, I do what I shouldn't. I lie next to her and put my arms around her like I've wanted to do all night.

Her back rests against my chest, and when she whimpers again, I whisper, "I gotcha, darlin'." I'm expecting her to open her eyes and turn around, but instead, she just sinks into my arms. So in the middle of my living room, I fall asleep with her in my arms. I wake during the night more times than normal, but when I feel her beside me, I go back to sleep. I get up before she does, leaving her on the couch as I go to the kitchen and start the coffee for her. Looking at the clock, I see it's almost six a.m.

I'm about to text my father when I see my mother coming up the back steps. I walk over to the door and open it. "Morning," she says quietly, but I put my finger to my mouth, then point over at the couch from the kitchen.

"She had a nightmare and didn't want to sleep in the bedroom," I say. My mother's face fills with concern. "She's fine now."

"I came over so you can go do your things," she says, taking off her shoes. I stand here, trying to come up with a reason not to leave her. My mother puts her hand on my arm. "It's okay. I have her."

After I nod at her, I walk back to my bedroom to get dressed. I'm hoping that Olivia is awake so I can see she is okay, but when I walk back out after getting dressed, I see she's still sleeping. My mother is sitting on the couch reading a book. "Can you text me when she gets up?" She just smiles at me, so I head out the door and make my way over to the barn.

Walking into the barn I had renovated six months ago, I find the concrete floor spotless, and the sound of my boots clicking wake a couple of the horses up. "Morning, fillies." Entering the kitchen right in front of the office, I start the coffee for everyone, then walk over to my office to turn on my computer. Another thing I did when I took over was make everything digital. No more handwritten notes, and no more writing contracts down—everything had a paper trail. Moving back to the kitchen, I fill a white coffee cup and take the first sip. Walking back to my desk, I make the work plan for the day so the guys know where they are needed and what needs to be done. After that's printed, I put it on the clipboard in the kitchen. I hired five more people since I took over from my father after I put in more stalls and have more horses here than before. Each farm has a purpose. This one is for training, and one is for mating. I opened one for lessons and that one is taking off through the roof. I also have one that specializes in rodeo training. I keep my mind as busy as possible and try not to look at the clock every two minutes, wondering if she's up, and if she's not, is that normal.

At eight thirty, I get a text telling me that she's up. They are making breakfast and I should head over. I don't know what I'm expecting when I get there, but when I walk in, I don't see her. My heart speeds up, and my eyes go around the room five times before my mother says, "She's getting dressed."

The back door opens behind me, and my father comes in. "Mornin'." He walks around me to my mother and bends to kiss her lips. "Sweetheart."

I'm about to go to her room when I see her walk around the corner, and my chest does something weird. I rub the middle of my chest, thinking maybe I have indigestion. She wears yoga pants with a pink sweater. Her hair is high in a ponytail, but the ends are curled. Her face is free of makeup, just how I like it. "Morning, cowboy." She smiles, but it's a fake one, and I have to say I hate it.

"Mornin', darlin'," I say. I wait for her gaze to meet mine again, but instead, she looks at my parents.

"Is there anything I can help with?" she asks my mother, who just shakes her head.

"I can set the table." Olivia walks over to the plates. "I wonder if Kallie is coming today?"

"She'll be over in a bit. She had things to do," my mother says. I walk into the kitchen to help Olivia set the table. I ignore the look that my mother and father give me when I do this, and no one says anything when we eat breakfast. The three of them talk, but I don't even know what about because all I think about is what will happen when she leaves. A knot forms in my stomach, so I get up as soon as I'm done and put my plate away.

"I have to go," I tell them. Looking down, I try not to look at Olivia, but I fail and glance at her before walking out the back door. Walking back to the front of my house, I get into the truck and head deep into my property. I have this sudden energy, and my mind is going all over the place. Stopping my truck, I go over to a pile of wood that needs to be cut. This should help to clear my head. I slide on the gloves sitting on top of the ax and then take a piece of wood. Moving it into place, I raise the ax over my head and swing, splitting the wood into two pieces. I do it over and over again until my muscles scream, but my head remains more confused than before.

I wipe the sweat from my forehead when I hear another truck approaching. "There you are," my father says when he gets out of the truck.

"Yeah, here I am," I say, grabbing another piece of wood. My chest is heaving from the exertion.

"Do you want to talk about what's gotten into you?" he asks, and I just shake my head. "It might be better if you do."

"Nothing to say, Dad. What do you want me to say?" I ask, taking another piece of wood and swinging the ax to make the cut.

"It's okay to be scared, son," he says while I toss the cut pieces of wood into the growing pile.

"I'm not scared," I say. I'm really not. Confused maybe, but not scared. "Why would I be scared?"

"Well, you almost lost her." Those five words cut me to the core. The five words I tried not to think about since I walked into that room. Those five words could have changed my world forever.

"Everyone almost lost her." I look at him. "Kallie, Mom, you." I point at him.

"This is true, and we would mourn her, but you ..." he says.

"But nothing, Dad." I throw the ax down. "She's just here until it's safe to go home, and then she's going home." Just saying the words causes my stomach to burn, and I get that feeling again in my chest. This time, though, it's followed with dread and pressure. "I need to finish this," I say, and he doesn't say anything more to me. He walks back to his truck, and only when he's gone do I roar out in frustration.

Nine

OLIVIA

Last night when I woke and I was clinging to him, he brought me to the couch. When I saw that he was sleeping on the couch with me, I almost sobbed. This man is sleeping on a couch because I'm the bitch who made him not safe in his house. Lying there in the room with him, I felt my heart calm down, and the nightmare didn't seem so scary anymore. I suddenly felt so safe, knowing he was there, and was able to fall asleep. When I opened my eyes this morning, I don't know why I was expecting to see him. I also don't know why it bothered me when I didn't see him.

"Good morning, beautiful girl," she says from the kitchen while she cooks breakfast.

"Morning," I say, getting up, trying not to do it too fast so my head doesn't spin.

"How are you feeling this morning?" she asks, and I just smile at her. The last thing I want to do is worry her again. "I was scared that you would wake up when I covered you up."

"You covered me up?" I ask, and I need to walk away as my stomach starts to flip.

"Well, the blanket was off you a bit, so I just made sure you weren't cold." I look at her while she smiles as if she just did what everyone else would do. Not once did my mother ever cover me for anything. She would leave me sleeping on the couch and have someone else carry me to my room and tuck me in, and even at that, the people did it because they were paid to do it.

"You are one of a kind," I say, smiling softly at her. Getting up off the couch, I fold the blanket. "Kallie and Casey are really lucky." I pick up the stuff to put it away. I don't know where, but I'll at least take them to the room I'm staying in.

She shakes her head. "I'm the lucky one. Now go wash up, and I'll call Casey to come for breakfast." I nod at her and bite my tongue when I want to ask about Casey. I walk away, trying not to think about how different our lives have been. When this whole thing blew up, my mother made one phone call to tell me not to reach out to her until it blew over. She didn't rush to my side, and she didn't send a lawyer for me. She did nothing, which just made me cement the decision to cut her out of my life. *It's just me*, I think to myself. I can be okay with just me.

I put the stuff down on the bed and take my phone out. I make the call that I don't want to make, but I do it anyway. I have to get out of here, and the sooner the better. The call goes straight to voice mail. "Detective Gonzales, it's Olivia Young. I was wondering if you could call me back please. Thank you." I put the phone down beside me, and I'm about to get up when the phone rings. I see that it's an unknown number, so I don't know if I should answer it, but it might be the detective.

"Hello," I say, my voice soft and quiet.

"Ms. Young." His voice sounds like he just woke up. "It's Detective Gonzales."

"Hi, Detective," I say. "I'm sorry if I woke you." I close my eyes. "I didn't even think about the time difference."

"More than okay," he says. "Is there something you need?"

"I was wondering …" I start to say. "I'm coming back to LA tomorrow. I just want to know how safe it is."

He exhales a deep breath. "I'm not going to lie to you. There have been no more break-ins at your place, and with the man arrested yesterday, I don't think the threat is there anymore."

I exhale the breath I was keeping in. "Perfect," I say even though I'm not sure if I'm happy or sad with his answer. "Well, I will touch base with you once I'm home."

"That sounds good," he says, and I disconnect, tossing the phone on the bed. Heading to the bathroom, I wash the tears off my face that I didn't even know were there, and the whole time, I can hear my mother's voice.

"Stop with the tears, Olivia. Tears don't help anyone.

You don't depend on anyone but yourself, Olivia; therefore, you can never be let down.

Never let them see your weakness."

Breakfast is weird, and when Casey says nothing to me the whole time, I have to think it's because we're all invading his space. But by tonight, I'll be gone, and his life can go back to normal. As I watch him walk out of the house, I think I breathe a sigh of relief. But then the minute I can't see him, my heart speeds back up. My eyes roam around the room frantically, looking around to make sure I can see everything in case someone comes to us.

When Kallie comes in an hour later, Charlotte leaves. "Why does that face scare me?" Kallie asks while I laugh.

"Maybe because I haven't put on makeup in five days." I try to joke, but my heart gets heavier, knowing that I'm also leaving my best friend behind.

"We went to Cabo last year." She points at me. "And you went ten days without makeup," she reminds me. I try not to think about how empty my life will be without her, but it's fine. It'll be okay. Maybe not right away, but eventually, it'll be okay.

"The detective called me this morning," I say, and she just looks at me, waiting. "Okay, fine, I called the detective," I say, lifting my hands in the air. "Anyway, it doesn't matter who called who. What matters is that it's safe to go back home now that they caught the guy."

"I don't know, Olivia." She blinks away her tears.

"I can't stay here forever, Kallie," I say, blinking away my own tears as my stomach sinks. I feel like I'm going to be sick. "It's time that everyone gets on with their lives." I try not to think about Casey and him getting on with his life. He'll go back to being the hottest bachelor in town, but this time, I won't be stopping him from dating.

"Everyone is getting on with their lives with you here." Her voice is soft now, but then it rises just a touch. "Is it Casey?" she asks, getting angry now. "Did he say something to you?" She shakes her head. "Fuck him, you can stay with us."

I laugh. "No," I tell her. "He didn't say anything to me. I swear." I hold up my hand like Scout's honor.

"I don't want you to go," she finally says. She wipes away the tears coming down her face, and I don't even bother hiding mine anymore. "I mean, who is going to help you with taco not Tuesday?" She mentions the time I tried to make tacos, but the turkey meat I bought got stuck to the pan, and it was crunchy when you bit into it. "Who is going to make you watch reality television?"

"We can FaceTime," I say. "My life is there. My home is there." I try not to think about how I've never called anywhere home.

She takes me in her arms, and I try not to sob. "I'm not dying." I try to joke with her. "You know I can come visit, and you can come visit."

"Where are you going to stay?" she asks, and I shrug.

"I haven't stayed at the Four Seasons in a really long time."
I smile. "I thought I would stay there until I got a new place."
We let each other go, and I get online and book my flight
home. The whole time, I ignore all the emotion coming out
of me.

She doesn't say anything to me, and we just hug each
other. When Jacob picks her up an hour later, she looks at me.
"I'm going to come right back, so we can spend the night
watching movies."

I nod, and when she closes the door behind her, I head to
the bedroom. Taking my luggage from the corner of the room,
I set it on the bed and open it up. I start packing my things. I
fold all my clothes, trying not to think about tomorrow. I'm so
inside my head that I don't hear the back door open, and I
don't hear him stomping his boots on the floor. So when I
hear his voice, I jump.

"What the fuck are you doing?" I look up to see that his
shirt is almost see-through from the sweat. His face is red all
over, and his pants are filthy. He looks like he just ran through
the mud.

"Jesus, cowboy," I say, putting my hand on my chest. "You
scared the shit out of me." I place the last pair of my pants into
the bag.

"Answer the question, Olivia," he demands. I can tell by
his tone that he's pissed, but for the life of me, I don't know
what he's talking about.

"Good news." I start talking, hoping my tone is peppy. I've
been preparing this speech ever since I made the decision this
morning to leave. "Since the guy was arrested yesterday, the
detective said it was safe for me to go back home."

He steps into the room, and I can see that his face is dirty
now, especially his forehead. "Which detective told you this?"

I try not to breathe in, and my heart starts to pound even
harder than ever. "The one working on my case in LA." I

ignore his look or at least I try. "I booked a flight out tomorrow morning."

"You aren't going," he snaps. "You don't leave until I'm sure the threat is over, and I'm"—he points at himself —"telling you it's not right now."

I shake my head, trying not to read too much into his words. It's not that he doesn't want me to stay because he wants me here. No, he doesn't want me to go because he doesn't think I'm safe.

"Cowboy." I realize I'm going to miss saying his nickname. I'm going to miss him so much more than I'm admitting to myself. "I'm going to be fine. Besides ..." I look over at him. He's so handsome. I look at his arms and see what looks like little pieces of sawdust. "It's time."

"It's not time." Charging over to me, he reaches for the top of my head as he pulls the elastic out. "I love your hair down," he whispers. The whole time, I'm standing here, holding my breath. I don't even realize that I'm not breathing as I take him in, and when I do, I smell him all around me. He smells of trees and the woods; he smells perfect. He threads his fingers into my hair, and my hands move to his hips. His eyes go darker as he gets close to me. "It's not time," he says again, but this time in a whisper. "It's not time." His face comes closer this time, and I can feel his breath on me. My heart speeds up, and I wait for it. It's what I've been waiting for what feels like my whole life. It's also something I know I'll remember, if only just once.

"Darlin'." When he says my nickname, his lips come so close to mine, but then the phone in his pocket rings. We both look at each other, waiting for the ringing to stop as my heart beats faster and faster. I want to get on my tippy toes this time and just take the kiss he wants to give me. When his phone rings again with a strange ringtone, he drops his hands this time, and I try not to let it hurt.

I tell myself it's for the best. It's better this way. He answers, barking out, "What?" He listens to whoever is on the line, and when his eyes fly to mine, I see something in his gaze. "Find out." He hangs up the phone and then his eyes go down before he glances up at me again. For the second or maybe for the third time, my life is changed. "Your attacker was just found dead in his cell."

Ten

CASEY

I say the words I know will change everything. "Your attacker was just found dead in his cell." I watch as she looks at me, and then she falls to her knees. I'm not fast enough to catch her in time and watch as she howls out in what sounds like gut-wrenching pain. "Darlin'," I say, picking her up and carrying her out of the bedroom. She buries her face into my neck and wraps her legs around my waist as I carry her into the kitchen.

When I walked in and saw her packing, I went through so many different emotions. I was pissed she was leaving and then sad she wanted to leave. But most of all, I didn't want her to leave. I didn't want her going anywhere, and I finally admitted it to myself. This thing between us is there. In all this craziness, I've gone and fell for her on a level that is just ... I can't even come up with the words to explain it. When I pulled her hair out of the elastic and then buried my hands in her hair, it was as soft as I dreamed it would be. Watching her shield go down, I saw the softness in her eyes as the color got just a touch lighter. I was so close I could taste her, but then the phone rang. I wanted to throw it against the wall, but then when it rang again with Derek's ringtone, I knew something was wrong.

I place her on the counter, but her legs don't let me go. My arms go around her, and I know that I'm filthy, and she's probably going to get dirty, but I don't care. I'll hold her for as long as she needs me to.

"Darlin'," I say softly as her sobs are beginning to subside.

"Why?" she asks, voice cracking, and I feel her breaking down. "Why me?"

I wish I had the answer. I wish I could say whatever she needed to hear. I wish I could make all this go away. I do know one thing—I'll die before it touches her again.

"I don't know," I say. The front door opens, and I hear the sound of footsteps running through the house. Kallie whips around the corner, stopping in her tracks with Jacob behind her. I look at her, and she puts her hands to her mouth. Jacob just looks at me.

"You heard?" he asks, and I just nod my head.

"Derek just called me," I tell them. She peels her face out of my neck. She turns her head, but doesn't loosen her hold on me. And neither do I.

"Why don't we run a bath?" Kallie suggests, coming to my side and rubbing Olivia's back. "A nice bath." Olivia looks at her and then at me. "We can use Casey's big one." I see the look she had in her eyes right before I kissed her is gone, and in its place is the shield, and I hate it.

"It's never going to stop," she whispers. "Why can't I just be left alone?" When she releases me, I see the defeat in her eyes. I watch as Kallie takes her hand and walks with her to my bedroom. Only when I hear the door close do I look over at Jacob.

"I'll kill him." My eyes return to the spot I last saw Olivia. "I swear to everything, if I see him, I'll kill him."

"I'm going to pretend I didn't hear that," Jacob says.

Walking over to the cabinet on top of the fridge, I take out my father's whiskey. I open it, forgoing the glass, and take a huge gulp, letting it burn all the way down. "You may want to go easy on that."

"Fuck you, Jacob," I say. I know I shouldn't lash out at him, but he's the only one in front of me. My phone rings again, the ringtone letting me know it's Derek. I put it on speakerphone this time.

"Derek." I say his name. "Jacob is here, and you're on speaker," I inform him in case he has something confidential. "What did you find out?"

"From what I can gather, he was killed between one and three a.m. The cameras on his block coincidentally went off at twelve thirty and only came back on at four."

"Coincidence, my ass," I say, looking over at Jacob.

"The guard on duty says he did a check at one thirty and everything was okay. When another guard did a second pass through, he saw him hanging," Derek says. "I'm already running a check on both guards, but so far, everything looks clean." I hear him typing in the background.

"Everything is not clean," I say. "Check their debt history."

Derek then stops typing. "I think I know what I'm doing."

"Yeah. Yeah," I say, not sure I want to have this conversation with Jacob here. "I want to know everything about them down to the last time they took a shit," I hiss. "Fucking everything."

"I'm on it." He hangs up, and I take another gulp.

"You need to reel it in," Jacob says, and I glare at him. "You aren't going to do her any favors by flying off the handle."

I'm about to tell him to fuck off again when I see Kallie standing there. She holds the wall while she sobs, putting her hand in front of her mouth to muffle it. It takes Jacob two seconds to get to her. "I need water," she says, her voice cracking. "She needs water."

I open the fridge, and I'm about to take a bottle of water to Olivia, but Kallie stops me. "You can't see her like that," she says while she tries to stop crying, but her breath hitches. "She doesn't want anyone in there. Not even me."

I want to burst through the door, not caring, and then Kallie's hand drops from my arm. "I just put her in the bath. I had to peel her off the floor. I've never ever ..." She swallows. "She's never been like this."

"Go back in there," I say to her. "I need to tell Mom and Dad about all this."

"Casey." She says my name. "Don't do this if you aren't sure." She shakes her head. "I love you with all my heart, but if you hurt her, I won't forgive you."

Jacob must feel my anger reaching its breaking point because he kisses her, whispering, "Go take care of your girl."

"I'll be back." I walk out of the house, and if I knew she wouldn't hear me, I would scream out to the universe. I walk over to my parents' house. They are both sitting out on the porch talking, but they take one look at me, and they both stop. My father gets up first.

"What's wrong?" he asks. My mother is right behind him.

"The guy who attacked Olivia was found hanging in his cell this morning," I say. My father just looks at me, but my mother takes a step forward to go to my house. "Not now, Mom."

"But ..." she says. "Olivia."

"She's with Kallie," I say, looking at my father. "She was going to leave, thinking that the threat was over." I put my hands in the back pockets of my jeans, looking up at the pink sky. "I have to head back."

"Makes sure she eats," my mother says. My father puts his

arm around her, and I turn and make my way back to my house. When I walk in, I spot Jacob on the phone, and he looks up at me. I walk over to the counter, screwing the cap back on the whiskey, then put it back in its place.

Jacob hangs up the phone. "That was the FBI," he says. I glance toward the bedroom and knowing that I can't hold her is killing me. Knowing that she needs something and I can't give it to her makes me feel hopeless. "They are calling foul play."

"No shit." I shake my head. "What else did they tell you that we already know?"

"The guard who was on duty that night called in sick, and this was his replacement." Now I look over at him. "Yeah."

"I'll tell Derek," I say, taking out my phone and sending Derek a text.

Me: Guard was a replacement.

When I put the phone down, Jacob asks, "You ever going to tell me what it is you do?"

I want to laugh and shake my head, but then I spot Kallie. She's wearing my shorts and a shirt. "What happened?" She shakes her head. Tears stream down her face, and she looks so helpless. "I got in the tub to hold her because she was shaking so bad." My hands clench into fists. "I put her in your bed. She was so out of it that she didn't even realize it."

"I got it," I say. She looks at Jacob, who walks to her and envelops her in his arms.

"If you need us, all you have to do is call," Jacob says and carries Kallie out as she cries in his arms. I walk to my bedroom and find her lying on her side in the middle of my bed. I walk quietly over to her, trying not to wake her. I want to lean down and kiss her head, but I don't. Instead, I walk into the bathroom, and I see water everywhere. After I put towels down, I start the shower. For the second day in a row, I take a fast shower, just making sure I wash off the dirt.

I keep the door open to listen for her, and when I'm slipping on my shorts, the sound of her screaming makes me rush back into my room. Standing in the middle of the room, she's shaking like a leaf while tears streak down her face and her chest heaves as she gasps for air. Her eyes are wide, and the fear in them breaks me. I grab her around her waist and pick her up, carrying her back to my bed.

"Darlin'," I whisper when she buries her face in my neck, and I feel her tears seeping into my skin. "It's okay. I'm here." I kiss the top of her head, and she clings to me tighter, but I lay her back down in my bed. Grabbing the water bottle on the nightstand, I take the cap off for her and hand it to her. "You need to take a sip of water."

Her hands come up, but she's still shaking so badly that she can't even hold the bottle. I bring the bottle to her lips, and she takes a little sip, then looks at me. "I'm ..." she starts to say. "I have." When she looks down, I see that the fear is going away, but something else is creeping in. "It was just a nightmare."

I push her hair away from her tear-streaked face, and her breathing slowly returns to normal. "There you go," I whisper. "Just breathe."

"They took me," she says softly, and my blood starts to boil. "When they arrested him, I was there. Wrong place at the wrong time." I watch her look down, and she finishes the story. "I was returning his stuff. I should have had it couriered over, but I wanted to have one last look at him and maybe see what I thought was there."

She shakes her head, but her eyes never meet mine. She sits on my bed, and my hands are on both sides of her legs while she talks. I want to hold her in my arms while she tells this story, but I want her to open up to me more than I want to touch her.

"I was there maybe two minutes before the commotion

started. Someone kicked down the door, and I was standing there with my feet glued to the floor. Even if I tried to move, I couldn't because a gun was placed at the side of my head." When her hand comes up and she rubs her temple, my anger starts to rise. "I can still feel the cold metal placed there." Her eyes meet mine, and I see the turmoil in them. It's clear for everyone to see. It's clear for me to see, and for once, she isn't guarded. For once, she is herself.

"He pushed me forward." One of my hands forms a fist. "Told me to get down. The words were stuck in my throat. I didn't know what was going on, and when I looked up, all I saw were black boots as they stormed into the house. It was almost like I was a part of a movie. They all had on headgear, and their guns were aimed, ready to be fired. I didn't even feel him pull my arms to my back, but I then felt the cold cuffs being placed on me. He took a hold of my arm and forced me to stand, and all I could do was watch. I looked over at him and saw he still had his gun out, and I have never felt more scared in my life. Dominic was dragged out of his bedroom. I expected him to tell them that I had nothing to do with whatever was going on, that I was not even with him, but he did none of that. He kept his mouth shut and didn't say a fucking word." She shakes her head, and I want to have four minutes with this guy. Four minutes and I would bring him to his knees. Four minutes of pure torture. "Actually." She looks at me now and then puts her head down. "He did say something. He said, 'bunch of fucking pigs.'"

"Darlin'." I lift her chin so she can see me. "You don't have to relive it."

"They threw me in a cell for fourteen hours," she says, and she starts to shake. "Fourteen hours without one word. Nothing. I sat in there for fourteen hours, and all I could do was relive my whole life. And trust me, nothing about my life is good enough to relive, let alone think about for fourteen hours. Every single time I heard footsteps, my heart sped up, and I got my hopes up that someone, anyone was coming for me. But not one person showed up for me. The only ones who came to get me were two detectives. I was taken to a small office, and all I could think was what if they don't believe me? What if they send me back to the cell, and no one comes for me?"

She puts her hand to her mouth before a sob comes out. I pull her to me, and I let her cry. Kissing her head, I want to say that I would have come for her. I would be there for her. I would have never let her sit in there for fourteen hours. I would have never let anything happen to her. But I swallow the words down. Instead, I do the only thing I can do. I hold her in my arms until she goes limp, the whole time making a checklist of the people who are going to suffer for all of this.

Eleven

OLIVIA

I feel so much heat around me, yet I can't help but sink into it more. I open my eyes, seeing the sun peeking into the room, and I have to blink two or three times before I register that I'm in Casey's room. As I look down at the arms around me, there is no mistaking that those belong to Casey.

Yesterday was pretty much a blur after he tried to kiss me. The whole night felt like a dream or, better yet, a nightmare. I went into Casey's bathroom and literally fell to my knees. Rocking back and forth, I repeated the same words over and over again. "It's never going to stop." Kallie cried with me as she peeled my clothes off me. She filled the bath, but not even the hot water could stop my body from violently shaking. Nothing could stop it. I was in daze, but I could hear Kallie tell me it was going to be okay. I could hear it, but I just couldn't come out of the daze. I didn't even try to fight her when she put me in Casey's bed. I just wanted to feel warm again. I wanted the cold that had seeped into my bones to leave.

"Morning, darlin'," he says from behind me, and I shiver when I feel his breath on my neck.

"Morning," I say, not turning around. I can't face him right now. Last night, I poured more of my heart out to him and told him about the nightmare that started this. Whatever little piece of dignity I had left was gone the minute he caught me in his arms and carried me back to his bed.

"How did you sleep?" he asks. I want to turn around and maybe wrap my arms around his neck. I want to go back to yesterday afternoon when he was going to kiss me.

"Better than expected," I answer. Honestly, I thought I would have nothing but nightmares after the first one, but in his arms, I felt safer than I care to admit. This isn't good.

"Are you hungry?" he asks, and I chuckle. He is his mother's son.

"A little." Turning around in his arms, I come face-to-face with his bare chest. I look up into his blue eyes when my stomach decides that it's time to eat. Letting out the biggest rumble that I've ever heard, it cuts the tension, and we both laugh now.

"If my mother was here," he starts saying, and I like when his voice is soft. My hands go to his chest, and his smile goes away. The two of us are so close, but he pulls me even closer with one hand around my shoulder and the other around my waist.

"It's just me and you," I say, and I don't know why my stomach is going nuts. I don't know why I'm so scared for this one kiss. I've kissed a man before, but I just haven't experienced the whole belly flutters with clammy hands.

"It's just me and you," he whispers. He lowers his head, and right before his lips touch mine, we hear a soft knock. I roll my lips while he groans. He looks at me one last time before rolling out of bed and storming out of the room.

"Yeah, Mom." When I hear him, I pull the covers aside and sit up. I'm wearing pants and a shirt, but I am still going to be coming out of Casey's room. Even though nothing happened, I don't know if she'll think something happened. I'm still contemplating whether to go out there when I see Casey standing in the doorway.

"Are you okay?" He looks worried.

"Yeah," I say softly. "I'm fine. I just ..." I look down at my hands. "I didn't want your mom to think I spent the night with you."

"You live here." He walks over to me, squatting down in front of me, and takes my hands in his.

"It's just I didn't want her to think ..." I shake my head. "That I slept with you." Looking at him, all I can think of is cupping his face and kissing him. I lift one of my hands to his face, and the stubble stings my hand just a touch as my thumb rubs his cheek. "Yesterday," I say, "was one of the worst days of my life." I shake my head. "I mean, the past month has pretty much been the worst ever." I smile just a touch. "But when you took my face into your hands, and I thought you were going to kiss me, I forgot." He just looks at me, his eyes going a light shade of blue. It's the blue you can get lost in; a color blue you can look at every day for the rest of your life and never get tired of. "For one second, I forgot my life was in an uproar. I forgot everything."

"Darlin'." He says my nickname, and I smile. He leans up, and I wait for the kiss. I wait for it, holding my breath, and right before his lips touch mine, the sound of an alarm fills the house, and my body starts to shake. Looking around frantically, I have the sudden urge to run and hide.

"It's okay," he says. The alarm silences, but the tears are now coming. My heart pounds so hard in my chest that I think the whole world can hear it. "It's just Kallie." Kallie comes into the room.

"Jesus Christ," she huffs. "Why the fuck is this place wired up like Fort Knox?" she asks and then sees me with tears running down my face. "I'm so sorry I scared you."

"It's fine," I say, shaking my head. "I just ..."

"Kallie, why don't you go put the coffee on?" Casey suggests as his hands still hold mine. She looks at me and then walks out. "I promise you," he says, letting one of my hands go to wipe away the tear rolling down my face. "Tomorrow, you won't shed a tear." I don't tell him not to make promises because I haven't had one promise stick. No one has ever made a promise and kept it. Even when I was four and my mother promised to take me to McDonald's if I got first place in the pageant. After I won, she smiled for pictures, pretending she was the perfect mother, then made me grilled chicken and steamed veggies because it looked like I was getting a muffin top. I learned then and there that promises were just a ploy.

"Coffee is ready. Mom is coming, so stop smooching and come out here!" Kallie yells, and I smile.

"We should go," I say, standing. He drops my other hand now, and when I go to walk around him, he stops me.

"I'm also going to promise that before tonight is over, I'm going to kiss you, Olivia," he says, and just the way he says it, my heart speeds up for a different reason. "I'm going to close the door, and if I have to barricade us in a room, I will. This kiss is going to happen."

I swallow, trying to make a joke about it. "Promises, promises, cowboy." He's about to say something else when the front door opens and then slams.

"I'm here." I hear Charlotte. I don't know what I'm expecting, but it's not walking out to the table being set by Jacob and Kallie while Billy comes in carrying two bags full of food.

"What is all this?" I ask. Charlotte comes over to me and takes me into her arms.

"This is all your favorite food." She smiles when she lets me go. I look over at Billy who puts the bags down and begins to unpack the containers.

"She's been up all night cooking." Billy shakes his head. "I told her it was too much."

I watch him unload the bags, and I'm speechless. The words stick in my throat. I want to say so much, but I know the minute I do, it's going to come out as a sob. Casey walks past us, going straight for the coffee. He makes two cups and brings one over to me. Charlotte leaves me to go prepare the plates as Casey hands me the cup.

"Breathe, darlin'," he says, and I look down.

"I've never had anyone take care of me," I say quietly. "Not once."

"Well," he says, taking a drink of his black coffee, "you better get used to it." I don't say that I can't afford to let myself get used to it. I don't think my heart could take it. "Is that fried chicken?"

"It sure is," Charlotte says. "Buttermilk just the way she likes it."

"This is ..." I finally say. Putting the mug at my lips, I take a sip, and the hot liquid burns all the way down. "It's too much."

"Oh, please," she says. "Let's sit and eat." Billy takes the seat at the head of the table, and Charlotte sits at the other end. I sit next to Casey while Kallie and Jacob sit in front of me. "I don't know about all of you, but I'm starved."

"Oh my God," I say. "Is that mac and cheese?" My eyes go to the platter, and Casey scoops some out for me. "And biscuits and gravy."

"Hot from the oven," Billy says. "You need to eat up." He points at my overflowing plate.

I sit at the table and eat until my eyeballs are almost out of my sockets. "Don't fill up now." Casey leans over, and when his shoulder nudges mine, just his touch sends my senses into overdrive. *This is crazy*, I think to myself. "Mom didn't take out dessert yet."

"I can't eat another bite." I turn to him, and our faces are so close, and I suddenly forget about everything. Looking into his eyes for just one second, I forget that my whole life has been tossed out, and that the wolves are chasing me. "I also think I need a nap."

"Are you tired?" he asks, worried all of a sudden, and he looks like he's going to get up and kick everyone out.

"I'm getting there," I say. Casey looks over at Kallie. The two of them share a look, and she just nods.

"Okay, let's get this cleaned up, so Olivia can relax. This might be too much for her." I'm about to say that it's not when I suddenly feel like I'm being watched. When I look over, I see that no one is there, and I'm looking out the window. Shaking my head, I remind myself that it's all in my head, and that no one is watching me.

"Are you okay?" I hear Casey from beside me.

"It's fine," I say, and then I look around again. "It's just, I feel like I'm being watched." His eyes look at me, and then I see him scanning outside. "But I'm sure it's just my imagination."

"Might be." His voice is tight as he pushes away from the table. "I have to go for a bit. Kallie." He calls her name, and she looks over at us.

"You need to stay with her until I get back," he orders. I'm about to say that I'm fine when another alarm goes off. Jacob and Casey both run out of the house this time. The commotion all around me feels like a dream as the doors are locked, and Billy stands in front of me with his back to me as he holds up a shotgun.

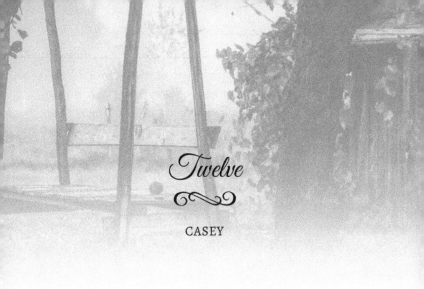

Twelve

CASEY

The minute the alarm goes off, I'm running out the door with Jacob behind me. "What the hell is that?"

"It's the alarm for the south side," I say, jumping into the truck and peeling off while I call Derek.

"What do you have?" I ask him. Rocks hit the truck as I speed to that part of the property, and for the first time, I'm pissed my land is so big.

"You have movement at the southern border. P17," he says. "You had movement of a man right before the feeds went dead."

"Fuck," I say out loud, speeding through the fields. "I want all feeds sent to my computer in two," I disconnect. "Are you packing?" I look over at Jacob, who just nods, lifting his shirt and showing me his gun. When I pull up to the fence where the feed cut out, I lean over and grab the gun from my glove compartment and then look at Jacob.

"Just so you know, I'm going to shoot first and ask questions later." I don't even wait for him to answer. Instead, I jump out of the truck and walk over with my gun drawn and aimed at the pole where the feeds went down. Jacob walks beside me, his gun also drawn as we get to the fence. Looking around, I see that the grass has been disturbed. When I look up, I see where the wire has been pulled down.

"Whoever was here is long gone," Jacob says from beside me as he looks around. I put my gun down and look at the wire.

"Cut right through," I say. "No accident there." I look around, and Derek's ringtone fills the air.

"Yeah," I say, answering after one ring.

"We got nothing," he says. "I can see a bit of an arm, but other than that, the guy was a ghost,"

he hisses. "He knows what he's doing, and he cut four more wires."

"I'll have them fixed in an hour. Meanwhile, I want cameras put on the roads that lead to my house."

"Working on it." He says something I don't know. "It's going to be done by tomorrow."

"Make it happen, Derek," I say. "He's getting on my land somehow. I want to know where it is, and I want to know what he's driving." I hang up and then look over at Jacob.

"What are you going to tell Olivia?" he asks. I look down and then look up at the sky.

"The truth," I say. "She's been lied to before. I refuse to be in that category." I turn and walk back to the truck, then look out toward the field, but I don't see anything in the distance. I study the side where the trees start to fill in again. "He's coming in through there." I point out to Jacob. "It's the only way."

"Or by there." Jacob points over at the small clearing on the side that I hadn't looked at. "It leads right to the side of the creek, and you can get onto the road by there." I turn the truck around, making my way to the road, and we see tire tracks.

"I'll call Grady," Jacob says. I nod and make my way back to my house.

When I pull up and walk into the house, my father stands there with his gun pointed straight at us. "Jesus Christ," Jacob says from behind me. "Can you put the gun down?"

My father lowers his gun. "Did you find anything?"

"Nothing. I need the wires at P17 put up again," I say, and he nods, taking out his phone and making sure someone gets to work.

"Where is Olivia?" I ask him, and he just motions to the family room. "They tried to get her to go upstairs, but she refused."

I walk past him and into the room to see my mother sitting on the couch next to Kallie, who is shaking her leg while biting her nail. Olivia lies beside her with her eyes closed. She must sense that I'm in the room because her eyes open, and she sits up.

"What happened?" she asks as my mother and Kallie look over at me.

"Someone cut the wire." Walking into the room, I sit on the coffee table in front of her. "They were long gone by the time I got there."

"I should go," she says softly, looking at me. "If I go, all this will go away."

"Over my dead body," my father barks out, and Olivia looks at him. "No way are you leaving here until I feel it's safe for you to." He folds his arms, and Kallie looks like she wants to laugh. Olivia just stares at him.

"He's sexy when he's assertive," my mother says. I close my eyes to block out my mother's words while Kallie groans.

"But I don't want anyone to get hurt because of me." Olivia stands now. "All of this is because of me, and I can't watch you guys—"

"Don't go off getting madder than a wet hen," my father tells her. She looks at him and then looks back at me, then at Kallie.

"I don't even know what that means," she whispers to Kallie.

Kallie leans over. "It means calm down." She gets up and walks over to Jacob, and he takes her in his arms. "We have to go get Ethan." She then looks over. "I'll call you later," she tells Olivia, who just nods. My mother gets up and walks over to give Olivia a hug.

"We will call later to see if y'all are hungry. I'll send Dad with some food," she says, and then my father looks at Olivia.

"I mean it, young lady." He puts his hands on his hips. "There is no running."

I look down, trying not to laugh at him being all in charge. Even Olivia tries not to smile, but she can't, and it fills her face. "Okay, Billy," she says softly. He grabs my mother's hand, and they walk out.

She sits on the couch in front of me, and I look at her. "My father was never a father." I just listen to her. "He stuck around as long as he could or as long as the money lasted." I sit here while she gives me another piece of herself. I sit here with the rage pouring through me. What kind of man just leaves a child? "Don't get me wrong, he did come back a decade later when he thought I was sitting on a nest egg of money. When he realized nothing was there, he was gone just as fast as he arrived." She shrugs, but I can see the hurt in her eyes.

"Then it's his loss." I push the hair away from her face. "It's his loss that he didn't see what an amazing woman you turned out to be."

Her eyes come up to look at me, and I lean in. "If I turned out so amazing, I wouldn't have to be hiding," she whispers.

"If you didn't do any of that ..." I swallow down the actual words I want to say, and instead, I say, "Then you wouldn't be here." I lean in a little bit more, and her breath hitches right before I finally claim her mouth. My hands go to each side of her head. My tongue comes out and meets hers. I swallow down her moan as she moves closer to me. I turn my head deepening the kiss. The whole time, her tongue rolls with mine. She climbs onto my lap and wraps her legs around my waist. Her arms go around my neck, and she presses herself into me. I wrap my arms around her waist and get lost in the kiss. The past couple of weeks catch up to me, and my hand roams up her back and into her hair. I grab it, pulling it back just a touch, and when she moans, I see her eyes are closed.

"Casey." She whispers my name, and I smile. My name on her lips makes me want to puff out my chest.

"Yeah, darlin'?"

"Is there anything that you can't do?" she asks, and I see that her lips are swollen from my kisses.

"Not that I know of." I laugh, and I kiss her again. Her legs get tighter around my waist, and my cock feels her heat. I'm the one who moans now as she trails kisses to the side of my lips and then to my jaw and then up to my ear.

"You are all that and a bag of chips, Casey Barnes," she says right before she nips my earlobe. I pull her hair back and attack her neck. "If you give me a hickey, I'm going to kill you," she mumbles. I think about what it would be like to have my mark on her neck, and it just makes me lose control. I suck in just a touch harder, and she moves away. "Don't you dare, Casey Barnes." She makes me laugh when she uses my full name. I'm about to go in again when my phone rings, and I see her eyes go from light to dark.

"I have to ..." I say as she untangles her long legs from my waist.

"I'm going to go lie down," she says. She walks to her bedroom, and I don't stop her to say she can use my room. The phone ringing again brings me out of my daze, and I see it's Jacob.

"Yeah," I say when I answer it.

"I just got off the phone with Grady. He saw a strange car around your property, and he pulled the plates."

I close my eyes and hold my nose. "Let me guess? It's stolen."

"Well, the plates have never even been in the system. When he went back, the guy was gone."

"What are the numbers?" I ask and get up to grab a pen.

"If we couldn't find them in my system ..." Jacob says, and I laugh.

"Humor me," I say, and he shoots off the number. I snap a picture and send it to Derek. "I'll let you know what I get," I lie.

"Yeah, right," he says. "How is she doing?"

I look back toward the hallway. "As can be expected."

"Let us know if she needs anything," he says before he hangs up.

I'm about to put my phone down and walk to her room when the phone rings again. This time, it's Derek calling. "Hello?"

"Where did you get this plate number?" he asks right away.

"Jacob got it from one of his deputies," I say. "Noticed a strange car. Ran the plates but got nothing."

"I would say." He laughs. "The plate must be code for something. I'm running it through a couple of systems. But I did get info on the guard who called in sick."

"Yeah?" I wait for him to continue.

"His ex-wife received a wire transfer of twenty-five thousand dollars," he says, "from an offshore account. The paper trail is going to need some looking into."

"This doesn't make any sense," I say and look over to make sure she isn't standing there.

"None of this makes sense."

"I was going to say the same thing," he says, and I do something I know I should have done a while ago.

"I need you to run the name Dominic Albano," I say.

"Why does that name ring a bell?" Derek asks.

"He was in the news the past couple of weeks." I don't say anything else.

"Didn't he take a fuck ton of money from his investors?" he asks, and I don't answer him.

"Is that what all this is about? What in the world are you doing up at that farm?" he asks, and I just shake my head.

"I think that if we find out what else Dominic is hiding, all the pieces will click into place."

"Got it," he says. "I'll be in touch."

I hang up the phone, then look out the window at the setting sun. I look up at the ceiling, and I pick up my phone one last time.

Me: I want a detail on the house. Round up the guys.

I don't care what Jacob says. I don't trust anyone but my guys at this point.

Thirteen

OLIVIA

My eyes open, and I gasp when I see that the house is pitch black. I sit up too fast, and when I lean out to catch myself, my hand knocks over the lamp on the nightstand. "Fuck," I hiss but not before I hear him running in the house.

The lights are flipped on, causing my eyes to squint from the brightness. "What happened?" he asks. I look at him, seeing that he was sleeping. One of his eyes is still closed as he gets used to the brightness.

"I ..." I lean down to pick up the pieces, and then I look up at him. He's in shorts again and no shirt. "I woke up, and I got up too fast," I say. "My head started spinning."

"I'll get a broom," he says. "Don't touch anything." He is back before I can try to pick up anymore of it. "I'll take care of this. You go sit on the couch." I watch him as he cleans up the mess. Walking around to go to the living room, I find he was sleeping on the couch again. I look over at the clock in the kitchen and see it's a little after midnight.

"I napped for eight hours," I say when he comes into the room with the dustpan filled. "Why didn't you wake me?"

He looks over at me when he throws out the glass. "Well, I tried at around seven, but you just mumbled something and then rolled over." He walks back to the hallway and puts away the broom. "And two, I think there is a saying never wake a sleeping baby." I put my hands to my mouth as he goes to wash his hands at the sink. "So I figured you'd wake when you were hungry."

"Well, now that you say that," I say. "Why don't you go back to bed?"

"And miss a midnight snack with you?" he jokes. "What do you want to eat?"

"I can prepare my own snack," I say and walk into the kitchen.

"Do you want me to warm up biscuits?" He says the words, and I look over at him and try not to give away too much. "Mom brought over some." He walks to the fridge and takes out a Ziploc bag with the biscuits inside. "She also brought over some apple butter."

"Did she put instructions on that?" I ask. Walking over to him, I take the bag from him, and there in the middle are the instructions. "Where do you keep your pans?" I ask. He looks at me, and I laugh. "You've never cooked in your kitchen?"

"It took me like two years to break it to Mom that I would be living in this house full-time." He opens the cabinets until he finds the pans he needs and hands it to me. "When the furniture got delivered, I swear I saw her wipe her tears." I place the biscuits on the pan and then start the oven.

"Aww, you're her baby boy," I joke with him. Something creeps into me, but I brush it away. I've never really wanted children, but the thought of protecting my own child fills my head.

"I'm not even going to tell you the number of times I've come home and found her cleaning my house. I had to sit her down and tell her to stop." He shakes his head.

"She's taking care of you, cowboy. You can't fault her for that," I say, thinking back to the one time I was sick, and my mother just brushed it off.

"I don't feel well, Mom. I have a sore throat," I said while I laid on the couch. Even getting up and going to the bathroom hurt.

"Oh, please stop with the dramatics, Olivia. You have a show to do." She said this while ripping off the blanket I managed to get on me. "The car will be here in five minutes. Pop some Advil and get dressed. I've worked too hard for you to ruin everything."

"I'll be back." He walks toward his bedroom, and I turn and open his fridge. I grab a couple of the muffins out with some of the apple butter and her famous strawberry jam. By the time he comes back, I have the muffins in the oven heating, too. "So what woke you?" he asks, taking plates out for us.

"I don't know," I say the truth. "I just opened my eyes, and everything was so dark, and then ..." I put my head down, ashamed to say that I was scared of the dark. He comes over to me, putting his hand under my chin and lifts my face so I'm looking at him.

"I'm sorry I didn't leave any lights on," he whispers, wrapping one hand around my waist, and I wait for him to kiss me. When he kissed me yesterday, nothing in the world could have prepared me for the kiss. My whole body lit up, my heart sped up faster than a speeding train, and my belly did the wave. It was the most perfect kiss I've ever gotten, it's a kiss I'll never forget.

He brings his lips down to mine and kisses me softly at first. "Your eyes change color when I kiss you." He kisses me again, only this time, his tongue comes out, and he slips it into my mouth. I'm not expecting to feel the same way again, but it's even more than it was yesterday. My hands go to his hips, and I turn my head to the side, waiting for him to take the kiss deeper. When he does, the beeping from the oven fills the room. I laugh out loud while he groans, then I turn to take the things out of the oven. Placing them all on a plate, I sit with him at the island while we eat. Neither of us says anything, and when we finally finish, and I get up, I see him yawning.

"Go to bed. I'll clean this up." He stands there looking at me.

"Only if you come with me," he says. My eyes roam the room as I look at the mess. "You can clean that up later."

"How about I sleep on the couch?" I say, hoping he goes to sleep in his own bed.

"Fine." He turns to walk away. I clean up as fast as I can and then turn on the little light over the stove. Walking over to the couch, I stop when I see him standing there with a pillow under his arm. "Get in." I just look at him. "I have to sleep on the edge."

"You don't have to sleep on the couch with me." Shaking my head, I walk over to the couch, then lie on my side with my back to the cushions. He puts a pillow next to the one my head is lying on, then covers us both with the blanket.

"Night, darlin'." He turns his head and kisses my lips.

"Night, cowboy," I say, putting my head close to his. I don't know how fast it takes me to fall asleep, but the next time I open my eyes, the sun is slowly creeping in. I look over and see that Casey is trying to get up without disturbing me.

"What time is it?" I whisper, and he looks over his shoulder at me.

"Six fifteen." He gets up. "Go back to sleep. I'm late." He walks to his bedroom.

"How are you late for anything?" I ask him as the sound of his laughter comes from his bedroom.

"I'm up at five usually and in the barn by five thirty." He comes out with his Levi's on while he slips into his white T-shirt. "I'll be back at seven, and we can walk over for breakfast." He brushes back his hair with his hands. "Think you'll be ready?"

"I'm ready now," I say. Tossing the covers back, I get off the couch. I don't notice that my shorts have risen, showing off my long legs. I've been told I have great legs, and they go on for miles. It's why Victoria's Secret took me. He looks at me up and down. "I mean, I can be ready in ten minutes." Running to the bedroom, I slip on my blue capri yoga pants and a sports bra with a midriff black shirt. I grab my sneakers and walk out to see him putting on his boots.

"You have a sweater?" he asks, and I look over at him in a T-shirt.

"Why? It's warm out." Sitting on the steps, I put on my socks, then slip on my shoes. "I'm fine."

"Darlin'." He stands up, and I just look at him. "You are walking into a barn with your skin showing."

"Ankles are not pieces of the body, cowboy." I shake my head at him. "It's just ankles. You know, in some countries, the ankles are considered the sexiest part of a woman's body," I say, tying up my hair, but my shirt rises, and he looks at me, shaking his head. "They are all covered from head to toe, but they keep their ankles out."

"You don't say?" he says from beside me. Our hands graze while we walk, and his pinky reaches out to hold mine. The rest of the walk to the barn is quiet. I listen to the sounds of birds in the distance, and I swear it's the calmest place in the world.

When we get to the barn, he opens the doors. "Welcome to my office," he says. Walking into the barn, I see it looks almost new. I follow him as he walks into the little kitchen to start the coffee. "Want to see Lady Princess?" he asks, and I nod as we walk to the first stall. The horse sticks her head out.

"Well, hello there, pretty girl," I say, rubbing the front of her nose. She blows out, and her tail wags. "Aren't you a beauty?"

"Do you ride?" I look over at him. Something about Casey is that I can't keep my secrets from him. It's almost as if I know it's safe with him.

"I did when I was younger, and then it got in the way of other things." I leave it at that. I don't say that it got in the way of my pageant training, and the one time I came in second place, she sold my horse and refused to let me ride anymore. "I used to love it."

He walks away from me, but I continue petting the horse. When he comes back out, he is holding two cups in his hand. He hands me one of the cups. "Come sit in the office." I follow him in the office, and I don't know why I'm expecting to see a dusty office with papers all over the desk, but what is there is a brown desk with four huge monitors on it. Then another desk on the side with six monitors as it flashes to different parts of the farm.

"You really have it all wired up," I say, motioning to the screens. He nods while he drinks his coffee. Sitting in the chair, he reads something on the computer. I look at the pictures on the wall. Stepping closer, I see one of Casey all dressed up in a suit while he accepts some award. He's shaking hands with someone while holding another award in his hand in another picture. Then an old picture in the middle of all of them has him dressed in chaps and a white shirt that is covered in dirt. He has a cut on his cheek, and he's wearing gloves. His look is of pure anger, but he has a little smirk as he holds up his hand with the number one.

"What is this?" I turn to him, and he looks up.

"That was the last time I was on the circuit," he says. "It was a do or die situation, and that picture"—he points with his finger—"captures the after."

"Why?" I ask him. When he leans back in the chair, I shake my head, feeling I overstepped. "I didn't mean to pry."

"It's just ancient history," he says, and I don't say anything else. I don't know why it bothers me that he doesn't tell me. Taking a sip of coffee, I decide to go back to the house.

"I'll leave you to work," I say and duck my head down. I turn to walk out of the room, trying not to let it get to me. Trying not to let it hurt that he hasn't let me in. Why would he? Why should he? As soon as this is over, I'll be just another memory for him.

Fourteen

CASEY

"I'll leave you to work," she says, trying to sound like she's okay. She walks out, leaving me wanting to kick myself. I just wasn't ready to answer any of those questions. My stomach burns with the thought of her walking back to the house without me, and I'm out of my chair before she makes it to the barn door.

"Olivia." I call her name, and when she turns back, I hate myself for the look on her face. The look that she did something wrong when she did nothing wrong. "Come with me." I hold out my hand, but I'm expecting her to tell me to fuck off. I would have told me to fuck off. "Please. I want to show you something."

She walks back to me, and I see that her shield is up now as her eyes are a dark blue. "I didn't mean to pry." She straightens her shoulders. "You don't owe me any explanations, cowboy." I hate that she pretends with me. I hate that I made her feel like she has to pretend.

"Will you come with me?" I ask, pointing over at the golf cart that I keep beside the barn. "I want to show you something." She shakes her head and looks down, so I step into her space and put my finger under her chin. "Please." She blinks away the tears without saying anything, but she nods her head. I hold her hand as we walk to the golf cart. She gets in, and I drive it away from the barn. "All this was my father's," I say, pointing at the fence we are driving toward. "On that part," I say as we go through a small opening to the other side of the fence. "This was his best friend's land."

"Is it okay that we are on the property?" she asks from beside me as the wind blows her hair back.

"It is now since I bought it." She just looks at me. When we pull up to the barn that I just finished renovating, I turn the cart off, getting out, and she gets out with me. "I spent most of my childhood and teenage years in this barn," I say. "Well, not this one, but ..." I put my hands on my hips. "I trained for the rodeo over there." I point at the same fence that is there now. "Seven days a week. My father's best friend trained me. Then he signed me to be part of his team. I was on top of the world. If you wanted to be in the rodeo circuit, you had to be with him. He was the best of the best, and he also trained the best of the best."

"Sounds just like you," she says, and I look over at her. "To put your whole heart into it."

"It's also the same place I fell in love." My stomach lifts when I think about it. "Lorelei was his daughter and my best friend. Two peas in a pod." She doesn't say anything, folding her hands in front of her. "I had my whole life planned out when I was eighteen. I was going to ride the rodeo and then take over my family farm."

"Looks like you succeeded," she says, and I look over at the barn.

"It was also the same place she tore my heart out." I look over at her. "She didn't do it on purpose, mind you. I caught her cozying up to someone else when she thought I was busy."

"Oh, Casey." Her voice goes soft. I know she means it out

of genuine concern and not just sympathy.

"Yeah, let's just say walking in and seeing her laughing at me was not something I expected. I quit the next day, but her father refused to let me walk away." I think back on the conversation.

"You can't quit. I own you," he hissed. "You signed a contract."

"Roger," my father said from beside me, and Roger looked over at him.

"Don't Roger me, Billy." He spoke to my father.

"Double or nothing," I said, knowing there was no way Roger would turn down a bet. That was his vice. Not knowing when to bet or when to walk away. "If I win the next one, you let me walk away."

"There is no way you can win. It's the biggest one, and you are sitting at fourth place," he said. "If you lose, I own you for the next five years." I agreed and shook on it, my father looking on the whole time.

"Why would he do that?" she asks, shocked. She comes closer to me and holds my hand now.

"Because he could. Needless to say, I bet him that I would win, and if I'm honest, I didn't think I would, but when I went out there, it's almost as if I saw black or whatever. The only thing I focused on was getting my freedom."

"But you won." She smiles, and for the first time since I told this story, I can feel good about it.

"I did." I smile, and she turns, putting her hands around my waist. "Not only did I win, but when I found out that his farm was in the red, deep in the red, I bought it from him." She gasps in shock. "Yeah, well, when I showed up that day dressed in a suit, he was also in shock. He had no idea I was behind it."

"Look at you." She laughs. "Doing the whole mic drop scene."

"More or less. Then I came here and said my last goodbye to the barn before I demolished it,"

I say. "What I wasn't expecting was Lorelei to be here." For the first time, saying her name doesn't bother me. For the first time, I can say her name without getting angry.

"Casey," she whispered as she looked me up and down. Not the same man she left in this barn four years ago. Gone were my Levi's and T-shirt, and in its place was the custom-made suit I got for this very occasion. "I didn't ..."

"Lorelei." Saying her name still got me. She stood there in her own Levi's and cowboy boots. A checkered button-down shirt tied in a knot at the stomach with her black hair curled. If you didn't know better, you would think she was going to a photo shoot. "Good to see you."

"What are you doing here?" she asked, and I put my hands in my pockets. "And what are you wearing?"

"I'm here to take a look around." I walked in a circle. "Lots of memories in this barn."

"Yes," she said, wringing her hands together. Her lower lip quivered just a bit.

"That stall." I pointed at the one that had her horse in it. "It's where I first fell in love with you." I didn't wait for her to say anything. "It's also the first thing I'm going to rip down."

"What?" she whispered.

"You see, I own this now." I looked at her. "Signed the papers an hour ago." Shock filled her face.

"Dad said he was selling to ..." I shook my head.

"CBS Corporation," I filled her in. "Casey Barnes Security." I took one look at her. "That stall." I pointed back to it again. "It's also the place you broke my heart."

"I never meant ..." she said and took a step forward.

"Lorelei, I should thank you." I smiled. "Excuse me, my plane takes off in thirty minutes." I walked past her as tears ran down her face.

"Casey," she says after I say the part that I never told anyone. "She was the one who didn't deserve you." She puts her hands on my face so I can look at her. "She had the best man that she would ever have in her hands, and she let him get away."

"Darlin'," I say softly, but she doesn't let me say anything else. She gets on her tippy toes and kisses me. And here, in the middle of the place where my heart broke, it started beating once more.

"Thank you," she says when we walk back to the golf cart, "for sharing that story with me. I'm sure it wasn't easy." I don't say anything while we drive back to my barn. I notice something is off at the crossing, so I look around and see fresh footprints. I look to the right and don't see anything, but then I look to the left and see a shadow in the field.

Glancing over to see if Olivia saw it, I decide not to say anything when I see her gazing out at the horizon. Instead, I drive straight to my parents' house and turn off the cart. "Tell Mom I'll be back in a couple of minutes."

"Where are you going?" she asks while she climbs out.

"I'm going to just go close the barn door." She doesn't ask anymore questions, and when I get back to the barn, I run in and pull up the feeds from a couple of minutes ago. I watch frame by frame until I see the man. Wearing all black, he doesn't once look up. Instead, he stands there watching us. Then he takes a picture, and just like that, he's gone.

I pick up the phone and call Derek, who answers right away. "Yeah, I just got the information."

"He's using a phantom car." I hear him typing. "I have nothing on him. He keeps his face covered the whole time. I don't even have a shot of his eyes. But I'll work on it in the meantime."

"What else do you have for me?" I ask, and he gets quiet.

"How deep are you with Dominic Albano?" he asks quietly.

"Not at all," I answer truthfully. "Olivia was engaged to him. She broke it off."

"It's a good thing because this guy is beyond dirty," he says, my eyes closing. "From what the feds got on him, he will go away for a long time." He pauses. "But that isn't the worst of it."

"How can it get worse?" I close my eyes, pinching the bridge of my nose.

"A lot worse." Derek's tone is not to be mistaken with anything but bad. "He fucked with the wrong people. Not only did he borrow, but he also lost their money—their clean money. And you know nothing pisses off a mob like losing what he must have spent years to clean."

"Fuck," I hiss, shaking my head. "How much are we talking?"

"Thirty," he says, and my heart sinks. "He also owes them ten."

"How the fuck did he let it get so bad?" I ask while Derek laughs.

"The guy loved the private jet style. He also loved hookers and blow," he says. "He also didn't like wrapping it up. He has two kids that he keeps under the radar, but there are wire transfers every single month. Needless to say, their accounts have also been seized, and neither of them are happy."

"It just keeps getting better and better." I sigh. "Let me know if you find out anything else."

"Will do," he disconnects. I spend the next five minutes watching the figure over and over again, trying to see if I'll notice something Derek missed.

When I walk into the house a little while later, I find Olivia on the couch looking up at the ceiling. "What are you doing?" I ask, and she turns around and looks at me.

"I'm dying of boredom." She looks over, and once again, just looking at her takes my breath away. "I haven't been out in four days," she says. "I mean, out in public with humans." She puts her hands up, and I can't help the laughter that escapes now.

"Pretty sure my parents are considered humans," I say. She glares at me, and even the glare stirs something in me. I also know when she's sad or mad or anything besides happy, so I do something I know I'm going to regret. "Why don't we go out?" I can't stop the words before they come out.

She sits up and looks over at me. "Don't toy with me, cowboy."

"I'm not toying with you. Call Kallie and see if she wants to go to the bar. We can go out," I say and she starts to clap her hands. "Not late." I point at her, taking a sip of my water.

She gets up and runs over to me, surprising me by throwing her arms around my neck. My arms go around her waist automatically. "Thank you, cowboy," she says, kissing my cheek. She looks at me, and all I can do is stare at her. There is nothing I can say. Actually, there is a whole list of words I can say, but I have to keep reminding myself that she's leaving.

I break eye contact first and drop my hands from her waist. "Yeah, go call Kallie." She nods her head and walks away to the bedroom. Standing in the kitchen, I put my hands on the counter and hang my head. "Don't go there," I remind myself. "It's just going to hurt when she leaves." I shake my head.

"Kallie says she's in!" she yells from the room. "She said she's putting on her cowboy boots, and she's going to do some honky-tonk thingamajig."

"Great!" I shout back at her. "Just fucking great," I mumble under my breath.

Fifteen

OLIVIA

I can't stop the smile on my face as we walk to the bar. I look over at him, and once again, I want to stop and just stare. He is so handsome. I want to put my hands on his face and kiss him for making me so happy.

"If I don't tell you later on tonight ..." I start. When he looks over at me, I stop, and my heels sink into the gravel just a touch. Any other time, I would freak out, but standing in front of him right now, I don't really care. "I had a great, great night."

He steps closer to me with a smile, and my heart speeds up just a bit. "You are very welcome." I look at him in his black jeans and white T-shirt with his cowboy boots. It's what he wears every single day, and it should not get to me still. It should not make my heart flutter just a bit, and it definitely shouldn't make me think of taking the shirt off him. "And if you want to keep your jacket on all night." He leans in just a touch, and I smell his musky cologne. Shaking my head, the ponytail moving side to side, I look down at my outfit. I paired my white jeans with a black tube top and then wore my black mini jacket with it.

"Hey there." I hear behind me and turn to look over my shoulder at Beau. He nods at Casey, then smiles big when he sees me. His black hair is perfectly coiffed, his outfit—khaki pants and a button-down—very much like someone in politics. I wonder if he owns any jeans. "Don't you look beautiful."

I'm about to answer him when Casey barks out, "Let's go inside." He walks toward the door, making Beau laugh. The sound of country music is coming from inside, and the door opens as a couple of people leave. I look around and see that most of the parking lot is full.

We follow him in, and the country music fills the room. I stand here looking around to see if Kallie and Jacob are here, but I don't see them anywhere. I'm about to say something to Casey when I feel his hand slip into mine. He pulls me toward an empty table. About ten people are already on the dance floor doing a line dance. Wooden tables are all around the dance floor, and looking past the dance floor, I see the back room is full of people playing pool while others are watching.

"I'm going to hit the bar," Beau says. "Do you want anything?" I look over at the bar, seeing all the stools taken as Savannah stands behind it with a smile. She tosses a bottle up in the air and then pours it into the shot glasses in front of her. Then she walks down the line, grabbing a glass and filling a drink. Her black hair is perfectly done, and her blue eyes shine. I look at her, and even I have to admit that she is beautiful. Her son, Ethan, looks just like her and nothing like Jacob.

"I'll have a beer," Casey answers right away "And she'll have a white wine." I look over at him, shocked that he would order for me, and a little bit annoyed that he knows what I want, but then I look at Beau.

"And a shot of tequila," I say. Beau looks at me with a smirk, then looks at Casey almost as if he needs permission.

"Um, excuse me? If I want a shot of tequila, I'm going to get a shot of tequila."

"Well, then." Beau turns around. I'm about to bark at Casey when the door opens, and I see it's Kallie and Jacob. She has to stop on the way to us to say hello to people who they know and that is almost everyone in the place since they grew up here.

"It must be fun," I say to him while I watch them say hello to the people around them. "Literally knowing everyone when you walk in someplace."

I lean on the table as the song changes. This time, the beat goes a bit faster, letting some of the girls cheer while they do another dance that I think I can do, but in fact, I would need a lot of wine to actually do. I look behind the dance floor at the guys in back. About fifteen of them all gather around three pool tables.

"What in the hell is she wearing?" I hear Casey from next to me. When I turn back and look at Kallie, I have to roll my lips.

"I think that is her honky-tonk outfit." She walks over with her cutoffs, cowboy boots, and what looks like a plaid button-down shirt tied right under her boobs.

"Hey, sorry we're late," she huffs out. Jacob just pulls the chair out and side-eye glares at her.

"What is that?" I say, taking out what looks like a twig from her hair. "Is this hay?"

"No." She looks around. "It's grass."

"How could grass get stuck in your hair?" Casey asks, his eyebrows pinching together, and I throw my head back and laugh.

"You guys banged on the grass?" I say. Hitting the table, I'm still laughing at them. The crowd around us looks at us, and I just shake my head.

"Your lawn faces the road," Casey says with a grimace on his face. "Oh my God."

"We were technically behind the truck." Jacob leans over and takes Kallie's mouth. Then he whispers something in her ear, and her cheeks go pink. I'm about to say something else when a guy comes up to the table, and Casey gets up to greet him.

"Literally, it's like everyone knows your name." I smile at my joke. "*Cheers*. The bar? The show?" I look at Kallie, who shrugs. "You never watched *Cheers*?"

"Nope," Kallie says and stops talking when Grady comes in with Monica, the receptionist at the station. "Hey, guys," she says, waving at them, and the two of them walk over to us.

"Look at what the cat dragged out," Grady says, looking at Casey and then smiling at me. I look over just in time to see Casey just glare at Grady while he talks to another guy who has come over, this one wearing a huge black cowboy hat. I sit back just watching how everyone just melds together.

"I get why you left." I lean over to speak to Kallie. "But I don't know if I would have stayed gone this long." I smile, moving to the new tune that just started. Looking over, I see a woman in tight acid-wash jeans and a white tube top saunter up to Casey. My stomach falls, and I try not to let it get to me. He's been here his whole life, so it's only normal that he would have dated her. Or at least she should have tried. I try not to look at them, forcing myself to look back at the dance floor. But my eyes have a mind of their own, flying back to Casey and the woman.

"Hey there, Casey," she says, batting her eyes. "Haven't seen you in here in a while." I try to swallow, but my throat is tight.

The waitress comes back with a tray full of beers, ten shots of tequila, and a glass of wine. "Beau sent this," she says, and I look over to see that he is chatting and laughing with Savannah.

"So on the grass?" I say, picking up my shot of tequila and downing it. The liquid burns all the way down. "Bet that was itchy." I try not to look over at Casey and take in the conversation that I'm having with Kallie. But when I see that she put her hand on his arm and fakes a laugh, I grab another shot and down it.

"Are you okay?" Kallie asks quietly. I pretend I'm fine, but she knows me. "He isn't interested in her."

"It doesn't matter," I say. "I'm not here for long anyway." I take another shot. The chair next to me is pulled out, and Casey sits back down. This time, he leans over and grabs a beer, bringing it to his lips. I am about to look over at him when Beau comes back to the table followed by Jacob. Grady and Monica head to the back where the pool tables are.

"Why were you guys late?" Beau asks, taking a bottle of beer, bringing it to his lips.

"They banged on the lawn." I pick up my glass of wine, smiling when Beau looks at both of them and shakes his head.

"I just got a visual." Beau gags. "It was not good."

"Can we please talk about something else?" Casey says, making the whole table laugh again.

"How are you doing?" Beau asks, looking straight at me, and I just shrug.

"I've been better," I say. "But I've been worse, so I don't know which is worse." I avoid everyone's eyes as I look down and grab the glass of wine. I do not want to see the pity in their eyes.

I feel arms around my shoulders, and I'm pulled to Kallie's side. "Love you," she says. I just smile at her, blinking away the tears.

"Love you, too," I say, and I'm about to say something else when I spot a guy come into the front door holding a bouquet. "Damn you, Southern gents." The whole table looks over, and I hear Beau groan now.

"Who is that?" I ask as we watch the man dressed just like everyone else in the bar. His shoulders are broad, and a smile on his face lights up even more when he sees Savannah.

"That is Chase Peterson," Beau says. "Owns the new construction company in town."

"He's new in town," Jacob says. I look back over at the bar and see that Savannah is a little surprised to see him here. By the look in her eyes, you can tell she is faking her smile. I've had that look in my eyes for my whole life. "He just started dating Savannah."

"Can you count lunch as a date?" Beau asks, looking at us, and I shake my head.

"It has to be dinner," I confirm. "Anything before five p.m. is not considered a date."

"It was a picnic," Beau says.

"Aww," I say, putting my hands to my chest. "A picnic." I look at the table and see Beau glaring. "That sounds awful," I say, and he just shakes his head and takes another pull of his beer.

"How have you never had a picnic?" Kallie asks. "We live next to a park."

"Well, my mother didn't even want me playing on the grass, let alone sit down and have a meal," I tell them, shrugging. "Don't even get me started when I became a model. There was no time to do anything. So I missed the boat on that one."

"You guys need something more to drink?" Beau asks, getting up. I look at the table, seeing that two beers haven't even been touched, and my glass of wine is only missing two sips. He turns to walk away from us. "Why doesn't he just ask her out?"

Casey and Jacob both shake their head. "That would be too easy," Jacob says.

When a slow song comes on, Kallie stands up and looks at Jacob. "Are you going to dance with me, or do I need to get another partner?" she teases. All he does is glare at her, but he gets up. Casey follows, and I look up at him.

"Let's dance," he says, holding out his hand. I put my hand in his, letting him lead me to the dance floor. He wraps his arm around my waist and holds my hand on his chest.

"This is nice," I say, trying not to get too comfortable in his arms. "Being out with friends. Talking, joking."

"Yeah," he says, looking at me. "Sometimes it is nice." We move around in a circle. The dance floor gets more crowded, pushing us closer and closer together.

"Thank you," I whisper. I look around to see that eyes are on us, and it's not just for me. "For tonight. For well ..." My arms wrap around his neck, and my fingers go into his hair at the base of his neck. "We are being watched." I try not to smile too big. "But not by the men." I look around, seeing some of the women lurking around. "I know that your dance card must be full most nights." I try not to let it bother me, but just thinking about it makes my voice go low. "If you want, I could stay with Kallie for the night."

"Darlin'." He says my name and looks straight into my eyes. "I'm leaving here tonight with the woman I want to leave here with." I can't say anything else because of the lump in my throat and the fear that any words will come out with my voice shaking.

Sixteen

CASEY

I walk into my parents' house, looking around to see that my mother is the only one in the kitchen. "Where is Dad?" I ask, heading to the coffeepot to grab another cup.

"He is on his way down." She looks at me. "Where is Olivia?" she asks, turning back to the stove.

"Let's just say Kallie and she had a drinking contest last night." I shake my head, thinking back to all the tequila shots downed and then more showing up. It was the final straw when she took off her jacket and decided to try to line dance. I'm surprised I left with all my body parts intact since the single guys were walking around the dance floor like sharks waiting in the water to snap their prey. I'm not even going to think about how it felt watching all the men watch her. Jacob needed to remove the beer bottle from my hand before I broke it.

Then when we were in the truck, she kept slipping down, and her head landed on my lap. I thought for sure she would feel my cock under her head and know that I wanted her. But luckily for me, she soon started snoring. When I finally did get home, she didn't even wake when I placed her in bed, and this morning when the alarm went off, she didn't stir.

"Oh, dear," my mother says, getting the bacon out of the oven. "Should I go over there?"

"Nah." I shake my head. "I woke her before I left. She took two Advil and went back to sleep." I look out the window and then look back at my mother. "Do you think you can prepare something for me?"

"Depends, what is it?" She takes off the oven mitt and looks at me.

"Just a little bit of sandwiches and some fruit," I say. "Some wine maybe."

She looks over at me. "Some wine?" Her eyes almost twinkle as she taps her finger on the counter. "You want to take Olivia on a picnic?" She folds her arms over her chest.

I'm about to answer her when I hear my father coming into the room. "What is this meeting about?" my father asks. Going over to my mother, he kisses her neck, then grabs the cup of coffee that she made for him in the cup he always uses.

"He wants to take Olivia on a picnic." I watch my father's eyes. He looks up at me, then he puts his cup down and folds his arms over his chest. It is almost the same thing he did when Jacob came over to ask out Kallie all those years ago.

"Casey Barnes," he says, almost hissing.

"It's not what you think," I say, but even the words don't sound convincing to me. "She's just never been on a picnic."

"Okay." He glares at me.

"Can you just relax?" I say, putting up my hands. "I have to check the property, and I was going to take her out on the horse at the same time."

"Have a picnic with her by the creek." My mother tries not to smile. "I'll pack a couple of things in a cooler." She walks away, leaving me with my father.

"You know she's here temporarily," my father says, and I

don't need him to remind me. It's what I keep repeating to myself every single time my head goes there. "Unless ..."

"Unless nothing, Dad." I shake my head. "She's leaving, and besides, I don't have anything I can give her."

"You have everything," he says softly. "You just have to take the chance."

I don't answer him because my mother comes back in the room carrying a bag. "I'll be back at noon to get it," I say, and she just nods her head.

"Do you want anything to eat?" she asks, and I just shake my head. "Okay, let me know if you are going to be here earlier."

Walking out of the house, I head to the barn, making sure that the horses will be ready at noon. When I walk back into my house, I hear the shower from her room going. I walk over and start the coffee. I grab a pack of bacon to make, adding some sausage in the pan with it.

"Oh my God." I hear mumbled from behind me, and when I look over my shoulder, I want to laugh at her.

She is wearing a baggy shirt, and her hair is on top of her head in a towel. "Good morning, sunshine," I say. She just shakes her head, mumbling something while she gets on one of the stools, putting her head down on the counter. "Do you want coffee?" She grumbles, and I laugh at her. "Want a shot of tequila?" I get the stuff out to make a bloody Mary while she mumbles and then looks up.

"I think I'm going to throw up," she says. I place the bloody Mary down in front of her.

"Drink that," I say. She takes a sip and grimaces.

"What's in there?" she asks and coughs.

"Trust me. You finish that, and you'll feel somehow normal," I say. When she just looks at me, I realize I was wrong. Out of every time before this, right here, she is the most beautiful she's ever been. "If you finish that, I have a surprise for you."

"A surprise?" she asks, eyes opening. "Is this something I'm going to like?"

"I think so," I say, putting the plate of bacon in front of her. She mumbles and pushes the plate away.

"Finish that," I say. "And then go rest, and I'll come get you when it's time to go."

She finishes the drink and then walks over to the couch. Only then do I see she's wearing booty shorts, and it doesn't take long for my cock to get hard. Looking down, I head into my office and turn on the computer, trying to concentrate on work. Nothing but thoughts of her go through my head, and at eleven thirty, my mother texts me that the bag is at the barn. I push away from my desk and walk to the living room, finding the couch empty. When I look down the hall, I see that she is walking my way, and she looks semi-normal again in blue jeans, a white shirt, and her sneakers.

"You ready?" I ask. She nods at me and smiles.

"Tell me my surprise," she says, and I shake my head.

"Better if I show you," I say, holding out my hand. She intertwines our fingers, and I don't let her hand go when we walk out of the house and head across the grass toward the barn. My horse is waiting outside, and he is already saddled up.

"Thank you," I tell Miguel when he hands me the reins. I look behind to see that the bag is already secured. "I'm going to get on, and then I'm going to reach down and pull you up. Miguel will help you get on." I get on the horse, then I look over at her. She looks so happy; the smile on her face is everything. I put my hand out, and she grabs it, then Miguel grabs her waist and helps her on. She sits behind me, and her arms go around my waist. "Are you good?"

She leans against my back and nods her head. "I'm better than good," she says. I kick the horse, and he starts to gallop.

We go from my family land all the way over to the other side of the newly purchased land. The wind blows in her hair, and when we start to go around the back, I lead her to the creek. The same creek that Kallie always runs to, and the same creek where we found that guy lurking around.

I slow the horse to a walk and look over my shoulder. "You hungry?" I ask. She nods, but she doesn't move away from me. The sound of the creek starts to get a touch louder as we get closer. Once we pull up next to the rock and the open area, I get off the horse and then hold my hand out for her. She grabs me and gets down, then she shocks me when she rubs the horse's neck. "Hold the reins," I say. She holds them in her hand while I get the blanket out.

"What are you doing?" she asks when I walk over to the open area under the tree and unfold the blanket, putting it down.

"We're having a picnic." Her eyes go big, her smile lights up, and I swear I see a tear in her eye. "I figured since we were out." I walk over and grab the cooler that my mother packed and then look over at her. "You can leave the reins. He won't go anywhere." She drops them and then follows me over to the blanket.

"I can't believe you did all this," she says, kicking off her shoes and getting on the blanket.

"I wish I could take all the credit." I laugh, sitting down in front of her. "But Mom made the food."

The smile never leaves her face as she ties her hair up on her head. I have the sudden urge to lean down and kiss her face, forgetting all about the food. "I'm suddenly starving," she says.

I open the cooler, taking out the sandwiches Mom made along with a container of fruit and another of veggies, and at the bottom is the bottle of wine. "See, she knows you," I say, and she just laughs. She grabs a piece of sandwich and sits down. "How's your head?"

"Better," she says, chewing. "Remind me never to drink tequila again."

I laugh, grabbing my own piece. "I'll remind you only if you tell me more about you being a model." I watch as the smile fades from her face, and she just shrugs.

"Nothing much to say. I used to model, and now I don't," she says. When she looks down at her hands, I'm almost ready to kick myself for asking her. "It's not a secret or anything. I started when I was young, then finally, a couple of years ago, I just walked away from it." She looks at me. "Almost like you up and leaving the rodeo circuit. That was how I felt about modeling. I was doing it because my mother made me, and then I finally stood up and said no more."

"It must have been hard to just walk away," I say, knowing full well how it felt losing that little piece of me. "A piece of me was gone. It was just weird."

"But you loved doing the rodeo, right?" she asks, and I nod. "I hated fucking modeling. I hated everything about it. Getting on jets and living out of your suitcase and the cattiness about it. One girl I know ate only an apple for the whole week." She throws her hands in the air. "Seven days with one apple. Luckily, I had a great metabolism, but that didn't keep my mother from trying to pinch fat on my body. Well, when she did that, it was always a bad month."

"Do you still talk to your mother?" I ask, and she shakes her head.

"No." She grabs a grape and tosses it into her mouth. "When I finished my last runway, I expected her to be there. Expected her to be somewhat proud of the fact that I had the career I did, but instead, she tried to punish me by staying away. In the end, she punished herself because I've never been happier." She shrugs and eats more grapes. "I mean, I guess you can say my mother is the reason that I settled with Dominic."

"How is that?" I listen to her telling her story about how miserable her life was, and I want to make sure she never feels that way again.

"I don't know what love is," she says, and my heart and stomach hurt for her. "If you've never had love in your life, how do you know what it feels like?" She shrugs. "It's like I know I'll never be a mother."

"I get that feeling," I say. "I'll never get married," I finally admit to her, and she looks at me. "It's just not for me."

She laughs. "Cowboy Casey on the loose." I shake my head. "Adding notches to your bedpost."

I look down and then look up. "Hardly."

"You're not lying," she says softly. I grab a water bottle and take a drink, my mouth suddenly dry.

"Whatever this thing is." I point at her and then at me. "The one thing I can tell you is that I will never lie to you."

"Thank you," she says softly. "I think that is one of the nicest things someone has ever said to me." She looks down and then she looks up again, and I see the tears in her eyes. "This can't go anywhere," she says. "I'm here until it's safe, and then I'm leaving." I want to ignore the crushing in my chest. I want to ignore the fact that my stomach now burns, knowing she'll eventually leave. I don't answer her. Instead, I look off into the trees and pretend my heart didn't just break.

Seventeen

OLIVIA

I hear an alarm in the distance, and my eyes finally open. I feel him leave my side and turn to look over my shoulder at him. It's still dark outside. "What time is it?"

"Five thirty," he mumbles. "Go back to sleep."

"It's five thirty?" I ask him and lean up on the couch, not believing him as he gets up and goes to the bathroom. It's the second night that I've slept on the couch with him. Yesterday, I spent the day on the couch bored out of my mind. I tried to work, but when I finally got my computer out and the emails started coming in, my head started spinning. Kallie looked over at me, and she took my computer from me. She then went as far as telling Casey about it, and all he did was glare at me and fold his arms over his chest. Needless to say, that night we sat in the almost dark, and we made out. God, the man could kiss like no one's business. He kissed me breathless, yet I didn't want to stop. Even when my eyes got heavy, and I knew I would be falling asleep, I went back in for one more kiss. It was always one more kiss until I fell asleep without a care in the world.

I turn over and throw the covers off when he walks out of

the bedroom dressed in his Levi's. "What are you doing?" he asks when I stand and stretch. "It's early."

"I slept for ten hours," I say. "Ten straight hours." I shake my head. "I don't even think I dreamed."

"Well, if you go back to sleep, you can sleep twelve hours," he says, putting on his shirt. This time, it's a black one. I look over at him, watching as he pushes his hair back, and I have to take a minute before I move again. I'm used to my heart speeding up when I look over at him, but what I'm not used to is the flutters in my stomach. The itch that my hands get to walk over to him and hold his face in my hand and kiss him.

"I'll meet you in five minutes," I say. Walking back to the bedroom, I get a pair of pink yoga pants and matching sports bra with a gray off-the-shoulder shirt. I grab my sneakers, and I sit on the stairs while I wait for him. "I'm ready!" I shout back when I tie my hair up on the top of my head. He comes from the kitchen and looks at me. "Let's get the day moving, cowboy." I wink at him, and he shakes his head. We walk out of the house just as the sun is rising and the sky looks pink. "It's so pretty," I say, listening to the sound of our footsteps since it's the only sound in the air. "It's so peaceful." Our fingers graze each other, and just like every other time, his fingers entwine with mine.

"It really is," he says from beside me. "No matter where I am, this is always going to be home." I look over at him and wonder how many other places he has. When he took me out to the barn yesterday and told me about his ex, I was floored. Did it bother me that he loved someone else? No. Did it bother me that he got hurt? One hundred percent yes. I never wanted him to feel that hurt. He doesn't deserve it, especially when he loves with his whole heart. As he told the story, you could just hear how his heart shattered all those years ago. But then when he got to the end, you saw that it made him the man he is today, and no one can take that from him.

"You're just like an onion," I say right when we get to the barn, and he opens the door. "So many layers to you."

He laughs at me. "I'll start the coffee." I watch him walk to the kitchen, and I take a minute to watch his perfect ass before I walk over to Lady Princess.

"Good morning, girl," I say, putting out my hand, and she comes to me. The horse beside her sticks out her nose. "Does someone else want attention, too?" I laugh and walk over to the horse. Her brown coat shines under the soft light from her stall. "Good morning to you, too." I rub her nose, and she breathes out. "Now, now," I say, rubbing her side. "Don't be all cranky."

"She likes you." I hear him from behind me.

"I like her, too," I admit. "She's a beauty."

"She doesn't like anyone." He laughs. "She tried to buck me off her just yesterday."

"Well, maybe you need to listen to her for a change and not just order her around." I shrug my shoulders, then look back at the horse. "Isn't that right, girl? You need to be listened to and not ordered around."

"Do you want to ride her?" he asks. When I turn to him, I can't even hide the smile on my face as I nod my head. I feel like a kid on Christmas morning coming down and seeing all the gifts on my wish list.

"You see that right there?" He points at me. "That's the best smile you got." I look down and then up. "Your whole face lights up. It goes from your lips to your cheeks to your eyes." I shake my head, and he just watches me. "You're beautiful." His voice goes even lower, and I look down. I've been told I'm beautiful my whole life from as far back as I can remember, but the way he said it—the softness to his words and the way he looked straight into my eyes—is something I've never had. "Let's get you saddled." He turns away just in time for me to wipe away the lone tear that sits at the corner of my eye.

He walks to the side and grabs a saddle, then comes over. Opening the stall, he goes inside, and the horse backs away. "It's okay," he whispers, and she finally lets him tie the saddle on her. "There you go," he says softly and walks her out toward the front of the barn, holding her reins.

We walk out of the barn door toward the enclosed fence part. You can see from the worn grass in a circle how much the horses have been ridden in here. "Let's get you on her." He looks at me. I put one foot in the stirrup and pull myself up, without his help, and I'm happy that I didn't embarrass myself by falling on my face. "So you *have* done this before." He winks at me, taking her by her reins and walking her around the enclosed area. She walks perfect while he holds her, then after the third round, he looks at me. "Let's see how she takes to you, and if she's good, we can open it up and you can take her out into the field."

"I think she's going to be fine." I lean over and pet her while I whisper into her ear. "Isn't that right, girl? You're the boss, so you tell me where to go." It's like she understands me because she blows out again.

He walks over to the other white fence and opens it, the reins still in his hands. "If at any time you feel like she is going to buck you off, just say the word."

"Oh, a safe word." I wink at him. "Didn't think you had it in you, cowboy. I mean, I thought you did, but now it's going to be making out even better."

"That mouth of yours is going to get you in a whole heap of trouble." The way he looks at me, I know that he means every single word. I also know that what he's going to do with me is going to have me begging him to come back and do it again.

"I have to know. Is the saying 'save a horse, ride a cowboy' actually ever used?" He just glares at me. "I mean, I've never met a cowboy, so I've never actually had the opportunity to ask."

"You want to find out that meaning, then all you have to do is get ready to ride," he says, making my whole body tingle. I swear, this time I can't even hide the shiver that runs through me. I'm about to say something when I feel eyes on me. I turn around, thinking someone else walked into the pen with us, but there is no one. I turn to the right, and all I see are the heavy wooded trees and the little light that is coming from the trees. I turn around right and left and see nothing, but something is there. I don't know what it is, but I feel it. "What's wrong, darlin'?" he asks, and I turn to him.

I contemplate not telling him about it so I don't ruin the mood, but I know that I could be putting him in danger also. "It's the craziest thing." I start as I look around again. "But I feel like I'm being watched." I try to play it off by shaking my head and faking a smile. "It's silly, I know," I say, and he just nods. When I start to trot around with her, though, the feeling is even more; so much so the hair stands up behind my neck.

Eighteen

CASEY

"It's the craziest thing, but I feel like I'm being watched." She shakes her head. "It's silly, I know." My body goes on high alert, and I stop myself from doing the only thing I want to do, which is grab her off the horse and put her on lockdown until this shit is over. Instead, she trots off, and I grab my phone to send Derek a text right away.

Me: I want the feeds from the cameras surrounding the barn in five minutes.

Now here I am, watching the girl who has me all in knots, literally in knots. The need to keep her safe almost consumes me more than anything I know. "Thata girl," she says as she gallops past me on the horse. I'm impressed that Lady M hasn't tried to buck her off. She rides with ease, and it's the hottest thing I have seen in the longest time.

"How're you feeling?" I ask when she nears me. Her smile lights her whole face up again, and the only thing I can think is that I want to keep that smile on her face all the time.

"Amazing." Her voice comes out breathless. "I forgot how much I love riding."

"Then why did you stop?" I ask, curious about everything.

"My mother thought I spent too much time with my horse and not enough time with my pageant lessons." She shrugs. "It was more important to learn how to walk with a book on my head than to learn how to ride a horse," she says. At first, I think she's joking, but her face is serious. The smile is gone, and in its place, is the look she gets when she's sad. After watching her for the past couple of weeks, I know her happy face, her sad face, and her irritated face. I also know her smiles, and the one that lights up her face is my favorite.

"So after I pouted for three days, she sold my horse to make sure that my pout was gone permanently." I just watch her as she slows down from a gallop to a trot. "You are the best girl." She talks to the horse, and I swear the horse turns around and side-eyes me. "You are just perfect."

"Why don't we get her back inside, and you can ride her after breakfast? The two of us can go for a ride, and I'll give you the lay of the land," I say, and her eyes light up, and I want to laugh.

"Really?" I just nod. She gets off the horse and then holds the reins while she talks to her. "Let's get you some water and then get you some grub." She takes her inside, and I'm about to follow her when my phone alerts me that an email has come in.

To: Casey

From: Derek

Subject: You are going to be pissed.

There seems to be some movement in the trees by the barn. I don't have anything, but it looks like a shadow moving. I'm already ahead of you and getting the monitors up and on screen. I'll call you in a few.

Derek

"Motherfucker," I hiss out and then walk to the barn, the whole time looking around to see if I see anything, but I don't. When I walk into the barn, she is already getting the horse water, and she looks like she's done this all her life. But I know she hasn't. She must feel me looking because she looks up, and I see her cheeks are a bit pink.

"Hey, I made you a coffee," she says, motioning with her head to the kitchen. I watch her the whole time, trying to calm myself down. I want to ask her all the questions, but I know now's not the time. I want her to tell me about her life while we are sitting face-to-face, but I also don't want to ask her about her secrets when I'm still not sure I'm willing to share mine.

"Thanks, darlin'." I nod at her and walk over to grab the coffee when a ping comes out of my phone with pictures. I walk over to my office. "I have to answer an email before we head over to my parents' house," I say, and she just looks over her shoulder at me.

"I can go ahead of you if you're busy," she says softly. "Help your mom." I don't want to freak her out, so I just nod at her and watch her walk from the barn to my parents' house. The minute I see her open the screen door and walk inside, I turn back to my office and call Derek right away while the images load.

"Before you start." He doesn't even say hello when he answers. "When we detected this, we weren't sure if it was an animal or a person."

"Tell me everything." The pictures come on screen, and I can see why. The person out there is hugging the trees while he walks from one to the other, so it just looks like a blurred image until you freeze it for one frame and notice his hand on the tree.

"From what I could tell, he was there from three a.m. until five a.m. He stops right at the perimeter where it opens. Right now, I can't see what he is focusing on, but we are working on trying to clear up the image." I try not to freak out that he was there while we were sleeping. I watch the screen as it goes from one picture frame to the next. *He's trying to get the lay of the land*, I think to myself and make a note to put in some traps.

"Um, hello?" I hear Derek's voice. "You still there?"

"Yeah," I say to him. "I want everything locked down tight. If a tree leaf looks suspicious, I want to know about it."

"Will do," he says, disconnecting. Looking back at the screen, I notice he has a mark on his hand, almost like a tattoo of sorts. I zoom in, but the image is too grainy, so I send a message to Derek.

Me: He has a tattoo on his hand. Find out what it is.
Derek: Will do.

Getting up, I take the clipboard, jotting down things for them to do. I include notes on the traps I want set, and when I walk into the kitchen ten minutes later, my heart stops but for a totally different reason. Olivia stands beside my mother as she helps her make biscuits. Her hair is piled on top of her head, she has flour on her cheek from her hands, and she just looks so happy. I watch how my mother teaches her, and she follows directions. *This is what she deserves*, I tell myself. This happiness and these carefree moments are what this woman deserves, and I'll give them to her as long as I can. "Hey," she says softly when she sees me standing here watching her. "I'm making biscuits."

"I can see that," I say, and then I finally notice that my father has been watching me the whole time.

"Morning," I say, and he just nods at me. Breakfast is the usual as we talk about the farm and what needs to be done.

"I take it you canceled your business trip?" my father says. Olivia turns to look at me, and I glare at my father. "It's in two days."

"What business trip?" Olivia asks, and I want to curse, but I know my mother would not be happy. I also am pissed that with everything going on, I forgot about it.

"Nothing," I say, my voice tight. Looking down at my

plate, I see that Olivia is looking down, too, and I want to kick myself for making her sad.

"Thank you so much for breakfast," Olivia says from beside me, trying to sound happy, but her tone is flat. I bet if I looked over, she would have a smile on her face that was fake as fuck. "I forgot that I have a call with my boss this morning." And now I look up and see what I was afraid of seeing. The fake Olivia is back as she smiles at my mother. "I'll see you later." She then looks at my father. "Have a great day, Billy." She turns and walks out of the house, and it's almost as if I'm glued to my chair. As I watch the door close behind her, I can feel my parents staring at me.

"Ass." My mother is the first to talk, and when I look at her, she glares at me.

"What in the sam hill are you still doing sitting here when the woman has left?" my father almost shouts.

"What do you want from me?" I finally say, dropping my fork, and it clatters on the plate. "This is your fault." I point at my father as I get up. "If you hadn't brought up my business trip."

"I always thought you had brains to go with your good looks," my mother says, grabbing her coffee cup and bringing it to her lips.

"She's leaving," I now shout louder than I want to. "Eventually, she's going to leave."

"It doesn't have to be like that," my father says. His tone is so monotone it's just as irritating as when I was eighteen and he spoke to me. His voice never rises, ever. "Son."

"Don't son me," I say, putting my hands on my hips and feeling all these emotions run through me. I'm angry that she just left. I'm pissed that she's sad, and I'm irritated that I couldn't just say what it was about.

"Okay, fine," he says, leaning forward and putting his elbows on the table. "I'll just say this. That woman"—he motions with his chin toward the door she just walked out of —"deserves a man who is going to make her happy. Like really happy." He looks over at my mother, and she smiles at him. "She deserves a man who will take care of her and spoil her, and for the first time in her life, she needs to be put first before anything else." I want to say that all that is me, but is it really? "Actually, now that I think of it, you aren't that man." I glare at him. "If you were that man, there is no way you would still be here having this conversation when you should be running after her. But instead, you stand here with your head up your ass." My mother just laughs, and I turn to look at her.

"Dumb ass," she says. For the first time in her life, she's called me a dumb ass. "She does deserve better."

I don't even know what to say to any of this. There are so many things I want to say, but all of them lead to the same thing. I'm not the man for her, and my father is right. She deserves all that and more. She deserves a man who'll make her smile. She deserves a man who will hold her at night and wake her up with coffee in bed. She deserves to have a whole house full of children, and just the thought of her having a child with someone else cuts me to the core. Especially knowing that I can't give her any of that, and that's what cuts me the most. I shake my head. "You don't know," I say, and he just looks at me. "She's never going to be happy living here on the farm."

"You ask her that?" my mother asks, and I just look at her.

"She screams high-class city girl," I say, and then I shake my head.

"You won't know until you ask her," my father says, and I don't want to think about it. Right now, I think about the woman who just walked out of my parents' house and stormed over to mine, and I think about the man who was watching my house.

Instead of answering his question, I turn and storm out of

their house. Making my way over to my house, I jog most of the way. "Olivia!" I shout out her name and wait for her to answer me, and after five seconds, when she doesn't answer me, I call her name again. "Olivia!" I walk toward her bedroom, and I see the door open and the bed made. "Olivia?" I say her name, looking into the room and seeing the bathroom door open. "Olivia," I say a bit more frantic this time and run to my bedroom, seeing it not touched. My heart sinks when I run upstairs because I know she would never have gone up there after last time. My heart pounds so hard and loud that it's the only thing I can hear along with my heavy breathing. After I check the whole house, my hands get so clammy and my stomach drops when it finally sinks in that she isn't here.

I pull out my phone and call Derek, shouting at him when he answers. "Olivia is missing!"

Nineteen

OLIVIA

I can still hear his tone in my head while I walk out the door. I push away the hurt feelings that I have. My mother's voice is coming in loud and clear.

"What did you expect, Olivia? You are nothing but a warm body and arm candy for these men.

No one needs someone smart on their side. They need someone who can make their stocks go up."

I shake my head and try not to think about it. I try not to let my feelings get hurt, and most importantly, I try not to cry, but the tear comes out before I can fight it back.

It's almost as if I can see my mother standing in front of me, holding her martini glass and laughing at me.

"Stupid, silly girl."

I stop halfway to his house at the barn and decide to go see Lady M. I walk into the barn, and I see a couple of the workers who I've met over the past three weeks. I smile to a couple of them and then I see that one of them is mucking the stall that Lady M is in. "Hello there," I say to him, and he looks over at me.

"I'll be done in a minute," he says, and I just smile at him.

"Can I help you?" I ask, and he just looks at me. "I used to do this when I was younger," I say, and he just laughs.

"I can't see it." He shakes his head.

"Well, I can't prove you wrong by standing here and watching." I grab a pitchfork and loosen up the new shavings he just put down. When it's all done, he just looks at me. "I'm going to go get her some water," I say, going over to the hose and twisting it for some water. Then I carry the pail of water back in and pour it in her water dish. I walk over to her and rub her neck. "There you go, my girl," I whisper, and she just looks at me.

"She doesn't like anyone," the guy says and walks out of the stall.

"Now, that isn't true." I look at her again. "You're just selective over who you like." I'm about to say something else when I hear what sounds like five people storming into the barn. I look around, suddenly frantic, and Lady M must sense him because she lets out a high-pitched neigh. When I finally look out of her stall, I see that all the commotion was caused by Casey, who stands at the door of the stall and glares at me.

"What the hell do you think you're doing?" he asks. Just his tone pisses me off, and even if I wanted to answer him, he doesn't give me the opportunity. Instead, he just opens the stall and comes in, Lady M stands between us. "I've been searching for you."

"Well, you found me." As I walk around Lady M and toward the door of the stall, he grabs my arm, and in reflex, I shrug it off. "What's your problem?"

"My problem," he hisses out and then advances on me, while I take steps back until my back is pressed up against the wooden stall wall, and I can't move anymore. "My problem is that I couldn't find you," he says, stopping in front of me, and the only thing I can concentrate on is his chest rising and falling. "I've been looking for you, everywhere," he says, almost hissing, as his hands go on the wall beside my head.

"Well, not everywhere." I try to say it loud, but it comes out more like a mumble.

"Do you know how long two minutes is?" he asks, and I make the mistake of looking up at him. His eyes are so dark, they look black.

"One hundred and twenty seconds," I answer him, folding my arms over my chest. "Seriously, I don't know why."

"One hundred and twenty seconds." His voice is almost in a whisper now. "Can feel like your whole life when you can't find someone."

"Well, you found me," I say.

"Yeah." He gets even closer. "I found you." We stare at each other, and I'm not sure what to say or what to do. He looks like he has so much to say, yet all he can do is look at me. "I found you," he says again. He bends his head, and I hold my breath and wait for his lips to land on mine. Even though I want to push him away and say no, my mouth itches to have his lips on mine. To feel safe in his arms. "Don't do it again," he says right before his lips fall on mine.

My hands travel to his chest, and I could swear he does a huge sigh of relief when he claims my lips. He kisses me almost like it's the last time he is going to kiss me, and I have to be honest, it always feels like that. Maybe knowing that this thing between us has an expiration date I don't know of.

"Casey," I whisper his name breathlessly, and before I can say anything more, the sound of someone clearing their throat makes us look over.

"So you found her," Billy says, trying not to smile, and my face suddenly gets heated. I'm waiting for him to push away from me, but instead, he brings me closer to him and kisses my head.

"I found her," he says. Billy just shakes his head, walking away chuckling.

"That is so embarrassing," I say, putting my forehead down on his chest. His heart is beating as fast as mine.

"It's not like he caught us naked," Casey says, his arms hug me tighter than before. "But seriously." I look up at him. "Don't do that to me again."

"Well, don't act like a horse's ass, and I won't," I say, and he just glares at me. "Now I want to take Lady M out."

"Is that so?" he says with a smirk, and I finally realize that he is too good looking for his own good.

I push him away from me now, and he laughs. "Jerk face," I mumble. He puts his hand over my shoulder, and we walk out of the stall.

"Miguel!" He shouts at the guy who was mucking the stall with me. "Can you saddle down Lady M and my horse also?" Miguel nods. "We are going to have to get you some boots," Casey says, looking down at my sneakers that are now dusty and dirty.

"I didn't even realize they were so dirty," I say, looking down at my shoes and bending over to dust them off. "How could this happen?"

"From the looks of it, you just mucked a stall. There is dust and dirt and all that." He points at the shoes, then takes out his phone and types something. "Let's go."

We walk to the opening of the barn where Lady M is waiting, and beside her is a beautiful black mustang. "Is that one yours?" I look over at Casey, and he nods his head. "He's beautiful," I say. He smiles, and I could swear he puffs out his chest. "Can I touch him?"

When we stop beside him, he grabs the reins from Miguel. "You can."

I walk over to him and pet his neck. "You might be even better looking than your owner," I say loud enough for Casey to hear, and he just laughs. "If you buck him off, I promise to give you some extra treats," I whisper loudly, which only makes Casey laugh even more.

"Let's get you on your horse," he says. I walk over to Lady M.

"Hey, beautiful girl," I say, rubbing her neck. I put my foot in the stirrup, getting myself on the horse before Casey even walks over to me. Miguel hands me the reins, and I look over at Casey as he mounts his horse, flexing his whole arm, and his muscles come out more defined than before.

He looks over at me as I stare at him with my mouth open. "Better close your mouth before you catch some flies." He laughs and then his horse walks over to us. "You ready?" he asks, and I just nod.

"I'm so ready," I say as we make our way out of the clearing. "When are we going to ride?" I look over at him.

"We are riding, darlin'," he says, smirking at me.

"I mean, it feels like we are ninety years old and using a walker." I look over at him, and he shakes his head, laughing. "I want to feel the wind in my hair."

"Okay," he says. "When we go around that bend over there." He points at the fence. "We can open it up, but I don't want you to push her too hard or fast."

"Got it," I say. The minute we get past the fence, I kick her, and Lady M picks up speed. She goes from a gallop to a trot, and when she sees Casey's horse beside her, she speeds up, and at the end, both of them are racing away. The wind blows into my hair exactly like I want it to, and then I feel Casey look over at me.

"We need to get them water," he says, and I just nod as he leads the way to the creek. His horse slows down and so does Lady M. When he gets off his horse, he looks over at me, but I get off my own horse and hold the reins as I lead her to the water. "I've never seen her be that comfortable before," he says, looking at Lady M. "You know I rescued her," he says. I look over at him and then over at Lady M, my heart falling more and more in love with her. "She was skin and bones. They tried to train her, and when she wouldn't listen, they would whip her."

"What?" I ask, shocked. I lean over to her and hold her around her neck. "I'm so sorry, girl."

He looks over at me, and I look back at him. "I'm sorry," he starts to say, and I look at him. "For before. I shouldn't have."

I shake my head. "You don't have to apologize for anything." My eyes never meet his. "It's none of my business."

I hear him huff out from beside me. "Do you want to come with me?" Now I look over at him. "I have to go to Atlanta for business and ..." My eyes go wide. "It is only for two days, max three."

"You know I can stay with Kallie and Jacob for those days," I say, and I'm not sure if he's inviting me because he wants to or because he has no choice.

"Olivia." He says my name, and I look up at him. "Will you come with me to Atlanta?" The way he asks and the nerves in his voice are so apparent I want to laugh, but I don't have time to because he walks over to me and puts his hands on my hips. "I want you to come with me to Atlanta."

I watch him, and the only thing I can do is nod. "Good. We leave tomorrow morning." Leaning down, he pecks my lips. "Now let's get these horses back."

I don't say anything because I'm scared shitless that my voice is going to crack or I'm going to sound like a giddy teenager. So instead, I just follow him back to the barn.

Twenty

CASEY

"Are you ready?" I shout, grabbing my bag and walking out of my bedroom. "Flight leaves in an hour."

"I'm coming!" she yells. I see her walking out of her room, and I'm again forced to see why the two of us could never be. She looks like she just walked off the runway. She wears white jeans with a pink top, and a matching white jacket with leopard heels. "I'm ready." She smiles at me, and I see she has makeup on this time, and her hair is loose and curled. It's crazy that she went from mucking a stall yesterday to this catwalk version.

Seeing her ride Lady M at full speed made her so fucking sexy. I was in awe by the way she handled Lady M when she thought she was going to do something. Now she blows me away again, and all I can do is watch her. "Is this okay?"

"Yeah, darlin'." I grab my bag. She just looks at me now, and it's her turn to stand there with her mouth open. Gone are the worn Levi's and in their place are dark blue jeans and a white V-neck shirt with a leather jacket. I pick up my bag and walk out of the house, and she just watches me. "What?" I try not to smirk.

"You really are all that and a bag of chips, Casey Barnes," she says, walking to me and then turning to run back to the kitchen to grab her carry-on bag. She stops in front of me. "Now I'm ready."

I open the door for her, and she steps out and then stops. "Is that yours?" She points at the black Range Rover parked in the driveway. It's the top of the line with tinted windows.

"Yeah," I mumble and lock the door behind me, grabbing her luggage and loading the trunk with our bags. She stands there and looks at me. "It's just a truck," I say, and she walks toward me as I stand next to the truck. "I only use it when I travel or when I have a special day."

She smirks at me now. "Are you saying that I'm your special day?" She wraps her arms around my neck, and I want to say that every single day with her is special. But instead, I just shake my head and kiss her. I open the door, and she steps in, and I try to come up with the words to say that we aren't exactly flying there commercial.

"I'm so excited," she says from beside me. "Do you know where we are staying?"

"Yeah, I have the name in my bag." I try to hold off as much as I can, and when I make my way over to the private airstrip, she looks around in confusion. When we pull up, and I park the truck, I look over at her. "I'll get the bags." I get out of the truck, and she meets me in the back. I walk past the gate and head over to the private plane that is waiting. A little red carpet at the end of the stairs.

"Um, Casey," she says quietly from beside me. When I get to the plane, the flight attendant comes down the stairs as I start to walk up the stairs.

"Good morning, Mr. Barnes," the flight attendant says to me, smiling. "Welcome aboard. You can put your luggage right over there." She points at the side of the plane. "We'll have it loaded up right away."

"Thank you," I say and put down the bags. "Darlin'," I say to Olivia, who now just glares at me. I wait for her to walk up the steps. She puts her bag on the table in front of her and then sits down, not saying a word to me. "What has got you all in a pickle?"

"Don't you pickle me, Casey," she hisses. "We are in a private plane."

"I know," I say, shrugging off my jacket and handing it to the flight attendant who is there waiting for it.

"Would you like anything to drink before takeoff, Mr. Barnes?" She smiles at me, and I look at Olivia.

"Darlin'?" I call her, and she turns on her charm and fake smile as she looks over at the flight attendant.

"I'll have a water with lemon, please." She nods her head and walks away.

"See," I say, sitting down and pointing at her. "That smile right there. Fake."

"See that," she says, pointing at me. "Fake as fuck!" I try not to laugh, but I can't help it and put my head back.

"What difference does it make that I can fly in a private jet?" I ask, leaning back, and she glares now even more than she did before.

"You think I give a shit that you can get a private jet to fly you all over the place?" She leans in now. "I've flown on private jets." She comes in closer, and her eyes go from a light to a dark, and it's when she is getting all up in a fit that I kind of love her the most. It's the time when I want to kiss her until the light comes back into her eyes. "I've eaten caviar on private yachts in the middle of the Mediterranean," she hisses. "So I couldn't care less about this. I care more that you didn't tell me. You told me when we were by the creek that you wouldn't lie to me."

I'm about to say something when the flight attendant

comes over with her water and then looks at me. "We are ready to take off, Mr. Barnes."

"Thank you," I say, and then I watch Olivia as she looks out the window.

"It's not that I didn't tell you," I start to say, and Olivia looks at me. "It's just not part of who I am."

"How can you say that?" she asks. "Are you or are you not sitting on a private jet right now?" Before I have the chance to answer, she continues, "Did you or did you not drive us here in a brand new car?"

"It's not brand new," I say as the wheels lift off the ground.

She shakes her head now. "You just don't get it." She looks out of the window, and I see her blink away tears.

I get up and sit in the chair next to her. "Darlin'," I say her name quietly.

"It's fine." She tries to do the fake smile.

"It's not fine," I say. She looks at me, and for the first time, she admits that it hurts her.

"You're right. It's not fine," she says, and I want to smile taking her in my arms for admitting that she isn't always okay all the time. "I don't care what you drive or what you fly in. I don't even care what kind of house you live in. I care that you weren't honest with me."

"I never lied to you," I say. "Not once."

"No, but you omitted it," she says and wipes away a tear. "I've been omitted my whole life," she says, and I want to take it back. I don't want to be one of those people who promised to say things or omitted.

"Darlin'," I say, and not touching her makes my hand itch. "I've never thought of it that way." I reach out now and move the hair out of her face. "Have you ever heard of CBS Corporation?"

"Casey," she says my name. "Everyone knows who CBS

Corporation is. They are all over my computer when I log on as the anti-virus kicks on. At the bank when you put in your bank card and it spins on the screen." She starts naming every single place she's seen my name. "Unless you live under a rock, you have heard of CBS Corporation."

I take a deep breath and then come out with the news. "I'm CBS Corporation." I watch her eyes as she takes in what I said.

"What do you mean?" she asks, not sure of what I said.

"I'm Casey Barnes Security. CBS," I say again, and she looks at me.

"But ..." she says, her mouth opening and closing. "How?"

"Well, when I was eighteen, I started playing around with the computer, and it turns out, I was really good at coding."

"I don't even know what that means," she says, and I just laugh.

"Not many do," I say and now take her hand in mine, bringing it to my lips. "When I left the rodeo, I was lost," I say. "All I heard in my head were the words 'he's just a hick.'"

"Casey," she says my name in a whisper, and I just shake my head.

"I know it's stupid, and I know that you know the whole sticks and stones shit. I get it, but it's just, those words they cut me. *Just a hick.*" I say what I've never told anyone before. "I took a step back, and I wanted to be more than that. I wanted to be more than what people thought I would be."

"You are more than that," she says. I don't hear any sympathy in her voice. It's soft, and it's genuine, and it's everything.

"It was a stereotype. I was a cowboy, so I couldn't be anything else," I say. "Then one day, I'm playing around with the computer, and I'm creating this whole thing. I was a natural with it, and I couldn't explain it." I shake my head. "I broke into the government website in three hours." I laugh now when she gasps out. "I mean, I didn't take anything, but I just did it because I could."

"Oh my God," she says, and she puts her hand to her mouth.

"Yeah, imagine what my mom felt like when they arrived on my doorstep and asked to see me." She opens her eyes. "Yeah, well, needless to say, it's when they brought me in, and I showed them, and then I told them how to stop it. Which made me finally someone who wasn't just a cowboy."

"You, Casey Barnes," she says, shaking her head. "Even if you were a cowboy, that doesn't mean you are less of a man."

"I know that," I say, and she raises her eyebrows at me. "I mean, I know that now."

"There are so many questions I want to ask," she says.

"And I'll answer every single one," I say. She just smiles at me, and I finally smile at her and lean back in my chair. "Every single one."

"Where are we staying?" She leans back in her chair and smiles. "Also, I want to go shopping."

"So you find out I have money, and you want me to take you shopping?" I joke with her, and she rolls her eyes.

"Trust me, I don't need you to buy me anything," she says. The flight attendant comes over with a fruit platter and puts it down in the middle of the table.

"We should be landing in about thirty minutes," she tells us and then walks away.

"You're the first person I've ever told." I lean with my back against the window. "I mean, my parents know, and my COO knows." She leans over now coming into my seat, her eyes light and her smile bright.

"Thank you for trusting me," she says, and at the exact time I kiss her lips, someone is breaking into my house.

Twenty-One

OLIVIA

His lips touch mine, and his phone goes off like a siren. He grabs his phone and opens it, I can see the screen of the kitchen. But I have to look closely to see the black figure tearing through the house. "What is that?" I ask. The feed goes black, and his phone rings.

"Yeah," he says, harsh. "Someone is in my fucking house." He just listens and gets up now, standing there. "I want to send a message." He waits to listen. "I don't care how you send it. Send it to his lawyer, send it to the fucking warden in prison." Then he hisses, "Don't fuck with someone who can bury you."

"Casey," I say, getting up. He looks at me, and for the first time, I'm scared of his look.

"He crossed the line when he came into my house." He hangs up the phone.

"What?" I ask almost in a whisper.

"Someone broke into the house and trashed your bedroom," he says. I sit back down because my knees give out.

"What?" I ask, shocked. "But why?"

"I have no idea," he says, and his phone dings again. He

sits down and pulls out his laptop from his bag he carried on. He turns on the computer, and I see the feed from the house. I watch in horror as the masked guy breaks into the house and goes straight for my bedroom.

He tears the drawers out in record time, then flips the mattress. When he doesn't see anything, he runs into the living room, tossing shit over, and then he runs into the dining room that has all my stuff on it since I started to work in there. He makes the papers fly everywhere. I look over at Casey. "What the hell do they want from me?"

"I have no idea," he says as the wheels touch down. My hands shake when I start to get up, and he puts away his computer. He holds out his hand, and when I take it, we walk down the steps out into the sunshine.

"There he is." I hear a man and look up as he walks over to us. He's wearing a blue suit and has black hair with a salt and pepper beard. He smiles big, but I can't see his eyes since they are hidden behind sunglasses. "Holy shit," the man says when he looks at me. "Is that?"

He comes to me now, whipping off his sunglasses, and I see he has brown eyes. "It really is."

"What are you doing?" Casey says, pushing him away from me. "Derek." He calls him. "Get away from her."

"That's ..." he says, pointing at me. "Do you know who this is?" He looks at him and then back at me, and I put my head back, and I laugh.

"Hi," I say to him, putting out my hand. "I'm Olivia."

"Oh, I know who you are," he says, and then he slaps Casey's arm. "You have been holding out on me."

I just look at Casey, who is missing this whole thing, so I lean into him and whisper in his ear. "I used to be a Victoria's Secret Angel," I whisper, and now it's his turn to be shocked. "Also *Sports Illustrated*. A couple other ones also."

"What?" he whispers.

"When you said Olivia Young, I didn't put two and two together," Derek says. "I have to get you new cameras at home because, let me tell you, they did not show her in the right light."

"You're an angel?" Casey looks at me. "How did I not know this?"

"It's not that big of a deal," I say. He just smirks at me and bends his head and kisses me softly on the lips. "It's not who I am."

"We are going to table this right now," he says with a smile, and then I look up at him. "But tonight, or whenever, we are going to discuss this."

"Okay," I say quietly as he puts me in the truck waiting for us. Derek gets into the front seat, and Casey gets into the passenger seat.

"Where to?" He looks over at Casey.

"Headquarters," he says. I just look out of the window and try to ignore this feeling I have inside me. This feeling I don't think I've ever felt. This feeling of contentment, of easiness. It's a feeling I've never ever felt so I don't know if it's normal or not.

I don't know where we are going, but we drive into an underground parking area. When the truck comes to a stop, I unbuckle my seat belt. My hand is about to open the door when it's ripped open by Casey. He holds out his hand to me, and I'm waiting for him to drop my hand when we walk, but he doesn't let it go, and when we step out of the elevator, I stop in my tracks.

CBS Corporation is written all over the brown wall right on top of the receptionist desk. "Is this your office?" I look over at him, and he just smiles.

"One of them." He says hello to the receptionist, and when we finally make it into his office, it's the corner one with windows on all sides, showing you the beautiful Atlanta skyline. He shrugs off his jacket and looks at me. "Do you want anything?"

I just shake my head, then he turns and walks out of the room, leaving me with Derek. "I can't get over it," he says, and I laugh.

"It was a long time ago," I say, and then I hear Casey's voice over the intercom.

"Derek, stop flirting with my woman and get in here." My mouth opens, and Derek just laughs as he walks out. I, of course, have no idea what to do, so I follow him also, and I step into what can only be described as a new dimension.

The room is dim and almost black. Screens fill all the walls from top to bottom. In the middle of the room sits Casey, his hands going nuts over the keyboard as five screens sit on the desk in front of him. "What are you doing?"

"What he does best," Derek says, snickering beside me with a smile on his face. "Fucking shit up."

Seeing him in this role is so much different; at the farm, he's a dirty cowboy with a smirk that'll make you weak in the knees. Here behind a desk, with his hands going a million miles a minute as his eyes work, it's so much more intense. "Okay," he says, "I found him going in by the front door and then taking off from the side and ..." He turns some of the screens. "To this parked car."

"He knew you were gone and weren't coming back," Derek says. "He would have to know."

"That or he trailed me, saw me get on the plane, and then came back," Casey says. "Either way, he's in my house."

"Did you take care of that message?" Casey says, and Derek nods. "Perfect. I'm going to go check into the hotel," he says, getting up. "I also put a bug on all the feeds in the prison."

"Is that legal?" I ask them, and they both share a look.

"I'll keep an eye on it," Derek says, then looks back at me.

"Do you have a phone on you?" he asks me, and I nod, taking it out of my pocket.

"This can also be how they know where she is." He looks at Casey. "I'm going to see what is in here." He looks at me. "Are there any nude pictures on here?"

I roll my eyes while Casey growls, grabbing my hand. "Call me if you find anything," he tells him, and we walk out. "You don't have nudes on there, do you?" he asks, and I push him away from me. We take the elevator down, and this time, he gets into the driver's side. I look over at him when I buckle myself into the passenger side.

"Is this yours?" I ask him, and he just smirks at me. "You know, one of these days, that smirk isn't going to make my stomach flutter," I say the words, and just like that, I want to kick myself.

"I make your stomach flutter?" he says the words so soft, and I want to slap my hand over my mouth.

"No," I say, trying to cover it up. "I meant to say that your smirk isn't ..." I try to think of the words at this point, any word, and when he laughs, I just glare at him. "Shut up."

He leans over, and right before he kisses me, he whispers, "Good to know I'm not the only one falling." My breath hitches as he slips his tongue in with mine. His hands come to my face as he tilts his head and takes the kiss deeper.

"Casey," I whisper when he finally lets me go, and I want to say that I'm not falling for him, that I can't fall for him, and he definitely can't fall for me. But that would be crazy. It would be insane, it would be the phone ringing that makes my thoughts go out the window.

"Hello?" he says, and Derek's voice fills the truck.

"Did you get far?" he asks, and it sounds like he's out of breath.

"We are in the parking garage," Casey says, and I look over at him.

"Her phone was a hot target," he says, and Casey looks at me. "It's got tracking; it's got everything that a stalker would put it in."

"Did you know?" I just look at him shocked.

"How would I know that I have a tracker in my phone?" I shriek out. "Who would put a tracker on my phone?"

"I'm going to go out on a limb right now and say Dominic," Derek says, and then Casey punches the steering wheel.

"I should have known," he says, looking at me. "I was." He shakes his head. "What else did you find?"

"The hot spot was being tracked to someone else. I'm in the middle of dissecting it," he says. "I'll let you know what else I find. But, Casey, if he put one ..."

"I know," Casey says. "Email me whatever you got."

"What does all this mean?" I say almost in a whisper when he hangs up the phone.

"It means that he put a tracker on your phone so he knew where you were every single second," he says and then looks down. "He also knew what you were texting and when you were texting. I will know more when I read the report."

"How could he?" I say, my head spinning. "When?" I ask myself the questions that I'm sure Casey is wondering also. "I don't understand." *I will not cry*, I tell myself. *He has taken more tears from you than he deserves,* I tell myself. "I was so stupid," I whisper as Casey takes us to the hotel, and the whole time, I wonder what else Dominic is going to do to me.

Twenty-Two

CASEY

I pull out of the parking garage and look over at Olivia who has been silent ever since Derek told us that her phone was being tracked. It's almost as if she gave up in defeat, right after I told her I was falling for her. I shake my head. Maybe it's a sign to let me know that it will not and can never happen. We are like oil and water.

Meanwhile, I'm the one who overreacted when I punched the steering wheel, and to be honest, I've barely kept my anger in check ever since someone broke into my house and trashed her room. I know that Derek has someone over there right now cleaning it up and putting in the new system that hasn't even been out yet. I also know that he's running facial recognitions on the guy's face even though all we see are his eyes.

"Where did you want to go shopping?" I look over and try to pull her out of her head. "We can either go now, or we can check into the hotel."

She looks over at me and asks, "Why?"

I look at her and then back at the road. "Why do you want to go shopping?" Laughing, I turn back to her. "I have no idea. You tell me."

CHAPTER TWENTY-TWO

"No." She shakes her head. "Not that. Why put a tracker on my phone?"

I try to answer her question, but in all honesty, I have no idea what his motive behind it was. "I have no idea. Maybe he was scared of losing you."

"Losing me?" She puts her head back now and laughs. "Now that I think of it, he didn't even give a shit." I try to say something, but she just continues. "He was just like everyone else and liked having me on his arm. I mean, sure at first, he brought out all the charm. Brought me to Italy for pizza on a Friday night." Her voice is getting higher and higher. "Who does that? I didn't even like pizza. I like pasta." I try not to laugh, and she looks at me. "I mean, not anymore. Now, I like everything deep-fried and with butter."

"Do you now, darlin'?" I ask her softly, loving the fact that she loves what we gave her. I mean, my mother more than we, but still.

"I do," she says. "He destroyed my life. Literally destroyed it, and just when I think it's going to be okay, and I can get over it, what does he do?" I look over, and I don't know if she's asking me or telling me. "He does the only thing a swine can do. He fucking kicks you again, hoping you fall." She wipes away a tear, but this time, it's in anger. "Not this time. I refuse. My whole life I've always had someone who wanted something from me. My first memory was when I was on the middle of the stage and my mother was standing there right in front, making sure that I moved exactly how we practiced, and when I did everything like a trained dog, what did I get from it? Even a trained dog gets a treat, but I got nothing. Not even you did good. You should have smiled a bit more, Olivia." My hands gripping the steering wheel so tight they are turning white. "Who gets false teeth at five because Olivia, you look like *Jaws*." My stomach gets tight. "Do you know that she refused to have me in open toe shoes because my feet weren't pretty?" I don't know this person, but I hate her. "My feet, by the way, are perfect."

"Everything about you is perfect," I say, and she shakes her head.

"Be better, Olivia." She mocks her mother. "You can do better than that, Olivia." She looks at me now, and I see the tears rolling down her face. "I never want to have children because I don't think I am going to be a good enough mother." It's that line that breaks me. I pull over the truck, and she looks over at me. Getting out of the truck, I try to calm myself before I open the passenger door. But nothing could calm me down, so I unbuckle her seat belt and turn her in the seat.

"Look at me, darlin'." I try not to grab her too hard, but my hands grab her face to make her look at me in the eyes. "You are going to be the best mother I know," I say, hoping she hears me. "You," I say, and she looks at me, and my thumbs catch her tears. "You put everyone before yourself. You are caring and kind, and most of all, you have so much love to give."

"Casey," she says my name softly, putting her own hands on mine.

"Listen to me," I say. "You are going to have all the babies and be the best mother." Just saying the words makes my stomach burn. Knowing that eventually she'll move on, find someone who loves her and who can give her all the babies she deserves. "They are going to have the best mom. You know why?" I ask, and she just looks at me. "Because you're you, and that," I say, my voice going down, "is everything. You ..." My thumbs rub her cheeks as more tears fall. "You are everything." I lean forward, and I kiss her, a soft kiss. A kiss for her to feel everything that she should feel. I want her to feel safe, I want her to feel comfortable, but most of all, I want her to feel love. Even for a brief time. I try not to think about her getting married, and I try not to think about her pregnant with someone else's child. I try to live in the moment except I can't. I already feel her loss, and she's not even gone yet.

"Cowboy," she says, letting go of my hands and running her hand through my hair. "I was always told there was no such thing as a perfect man." She starts to tell me, and she looks into my eyes while she does this. The blue of her eyes going soft. "They were wrong," she whispers and leans forward to kiss the side of my mouth. "He does exist; he's just deep undercover." I try not to let her words get to me, but they do. They seep into my bones along with her touch.

"We should get you something to eat." I try to avoid her eyes this time and build a wall around my heart. Except it doesn't go up as easily, and I have a feeling the more time I spend with her the longer it will take me to get over her. She smiles at me, and I get lost in her once again. "What do you want to eat?"

"Anything you want to feed me." She winks at me, and I throw my head back and laugh. "Hint, hint." She laughs, and I shake my head and turn her around in her seat, closing the door as the sound of her laughter fills the air.

I walk around the truck, glancing over at her to see that she is looking in the mirror and dabbing her eyes with a Kleenex. "You look perfect," I say, and when she looks over at me her whole face lights up.

"You know, in all this time, no one has ever said that to me," she says, looking back in the mirror. "I was told I'm beautiful, and outstanding, exquisite, but I was never perfect."

"That's because you weren't asking the right people." I turn back and make my way over to the hotel.

"So does this hotel have room service?" she asks, and I have to laugh.

"If it doesn't, they need to rethink their prices." I pull up to the front of the hotel. I park the truck, and two bellhops come out right away.

"Welcome to the St. Regis Hotel," he says, and I hear a gasp from beside me.

"Sorry, it's not the Waldorf." I wink at her, getting out. One of the bellboys grab the bags from the trunk.

"Are we checking in?" the bellhop asks, and I nod my head.

"Mr. Barnes," I say my name, and he nods. "Your butler is waiting for you at the concierge station."

"Thank you," I say and look over to see Olivia standing beside me. My hand goes out to hold hers. There is no way I'm walking into this hotel and it's not known that she's mine or at least that she's with me.

When we walk in the lobby I look around and someone must have called them because someone in a suit walks up to us. "Mr. & Mrs. Barnes, so great to have you with us." I don't correct him and neither does Olivia. "I'm Diego, if you will follow me this way." He smiles at us and I nod following him to a secret hallway where a private elevator is waiting for us. "You are on the twenty-sixth floor. The penthouse takes the whole floor."

"Penthouse," Olivia whispers from beside me followed by a whistle. "Mr. CEO." She laughs and I look down at her as she leans over and pinches my ass. "You think you know someone and then poof. Millionaire."

I shake my head, looking over at the butler who tries to hide his smile. The elevator pings open and the butler waits for us to get out. "It's a two-bedroom penthouse," he says, and I look over to see if Olivia noticed, and of course, she did. For the past week, we've been sharing the couch. She follows Diego as he takes us from room to room showing us the master bedroom, his and her bathroom. The kitchen that leads to the great room and then finally to the private covered terrace. "Is there anything that you would like to eat?" He looks at me, and I just look at Olivia.

"I'm good with anything," she tells him and then looks at me. "Do you want a burger maybe?"

"Yeah, that sounds good." My phone pings in my pocket. I get it, seeing that it's a text from Derek.

"Excuse me." I look at them and walk out to the terrace calling Derek.

"Hey." He answers right away. "They just left your house."

"Good," I say. "Did they get everything done?"

"They did," he says, and then his voice trails.

"What aren't you telling me?" I ask him and turn to look over my shoulder seeing Olivia talking to Diego.

"They left a note," Derek says, and the hair on the back of my neck stands up.

"What do you mean? What kind of note?" I ask him, my eyes never having Olivia out of my sight.

"What the fuck does that mean?" I ask him and then see that Olivia is coming outside and the smile on her face goes away when she looks at me.

"What happened?" she asks, and I look down and wonder how I can say this.

I think about lying to her but then I will be like all the other ones and I refuse to be in the same category. "They left a note," I say and she walks over to the couch and sits down.

"What note?" she asks almost in a whisper.

I put the phone on speaker. "Derek, Olivia is here, and you're on speakerphone. She wants to know what was in the note."

"Um," he starts and I know he isn't sure what to do.

"The truth," I say and I watch her face as he tells her what he just told me and her eyes fly to mine.

"Okay," he says, his voice going low. "The sooner you give us what we want, the sooner you get to live your life."

Twenty-Three

OLIVIA

It's a good thing I'm sitting down because the words on the note would have had me on my ass. I shake my head, and my legs start to move up and down automatically. "I have no fucking idea what I have that they want," I tell them, almost shouting. "If I knew what they wanted I would give it to them gladly." I look up and blink away the tears. "I have no idea what they want."

"I know you don't." Casey comes over, taking me in his arms sitting with me in his lap.

"Is there anything else?" Casey asks Derek.

"Not that I can see," he tells him. "But we are looking into her phone and there was an application on there that I've never seen before."

"I don't really have applications on the phone," I tell them. "I mean, I have Instagram and Pinterest."

"Um," Derek says. "You have at least seventeen, and it was in a hidden folder."

I look at Casey. "I can barely get my computer to work, and when it doesn't, I do what every single other person does.

CHAPTER TWENTY-THREE

I shut it off and then hope when I turn it back on everything is working."

He looks at me. "You do not." The look on his face is that of utter disgust almost.

"I don't do computers," I tell them. "I'm a stylist. I style things. Then I walk over to Kallie's office and explain it to her, and she makes it come to life."

"I can teach you," he says, his voice going soft and I almost forget that my life is a mess. Almost. But sitting in his arms I know that soon this nightmare will be over and someone else will be in his arms.

"Okay," I whisper out and then Derek cuts in.

"I'll see you guys tomorrow, and if I get anything else, I'll let you know," he says, disconnecting.

"I have a dinner tonight," Casey says to me, and I nod my head.

"It's okay. I can stay, order room service, and eat in bed," I say with a smile. Putting one arm around his shoulder, I lean in to kiss his lips because I can.

"I was hoping that maybe you could be my date." He looks down, and if I didn't know any better, I would think that he was nervous.

"Really?" I play with him. "What does being your date entail?" I lean in and put my head on his shoulder. He puts one hand around my waist and another one over my legs.

"Well, it entails you dressing up," he starts with a chuckle. "Then it entails us leaving and attending a stuffy dinner. Where tech people will be."

"That sounds interesting and not at all dull," I say and lean in to whisper in his ear. "Does it end with me and you in bed?" I swallow down the nerves as I wait for him to answer.

"That sounds like something that can happen." He looks down at me. "It's definitely something I've dreamed of happening."

"Then sign me up," I say the whole time, wondering if I have anything that I can wear. "What time does this happen?"

"Six," he says, and I just nod. Diego comes back with our meal, and when I finish, I lean over and kiss him, telling him I'm going to get ready. I open my bag and take out the only two outfits I brought. I opt for the white off-the-shoulder long-sleeved lace dress that fits tight and ends right above the knee. I place it on the hanger and then take out my makeup.

The whole time it feels like my stomach is in my throat, I get ready. *This is silly*, I tell myself. I've been on dates before. I've been dressed up before, except this time it's with Casey. Casey, who wipes my tears and holds my hand to make me feel better. Casey, who is hands down the most handsome man I've ever met. Casey, who I've fallen for. Casey, who I'm going to have to leave when all of this is done. I apply my light makeup, not having to use any foundation since my face has a natural tan from being outside. My long blond hair is placed in curls, and when I slip on the dress and turn to zip it at the side, the zipper goes up easily. I sit on the bed and slip on the gold heels that have one strap over the toes and another strap around the ankle. I zip it in the back and get up, having time to look at myself in the mirror before I hear a soft knock. "Come in," I say, grabbing one of the gold chandelier earrings and putting it in.

The door opens, and he comes in but the sight of him stops my heart or maybe for the first time in my life it fills it so full I don't know what to do with it. My hand slowly comes down from my ear as I watch him wearing a custom-made black suit with a white button-down shirt. A black tie and on his wrist a silver Rolex. "Holy shit," I say, and he just laughs.

"Different from the Levi's?" he says and smirks, and I just shake my head and walk to him. His eyes go up and down. "You have a jacket."

"No." I shake my head. "It's too warm out."

"But ..." He picks up his hand, and his finger traces along the top of my dress. "Your skin is all out." His voice is going lower by the time he's done. His blue eyes are now a deep blue and in two seconds his hand is in my hair and his lips are on mine. Unlike his kisses in the past that have been soft and delicate, this kiss, it's hungry, it's all tongue and hands, and it's all Casey. His smell, his touch, everything about him. I don't care if he's wearing a three-piece suit or if he's wearing his Levi's, he's still the man who has crept into my heart.

"Casey," I whisper his name when he finally lets my lips go.

"I've never seen anyone so stunning in all my life," he says in a whisper as he leans down and kisses my shoulder. "Stunning." I put my hand on his cheek, the smile on my face so big my cheeks hurt.

"You clean up good, cowboy," I say, and he grabs my hand and brings it to his lips. "Now let's go before I do what I really want to do."

"What is that?" he asks, and for the first time, I jump without thinking.

"I want to save the horse," I say, leaning in. "And ride the cowboy." I kiss him under his chin, and I walk out, grabbing my St-Laurent light pink purse. I stop at the doorway and look over my shoulder. "You coming, cowboy?" I ask, and he shakes his head.

"I just need a minute," he says and I roll my lips.

"If it helps you at all." I look at him. "I'm not wearing panties," I whisper and walk out of the room, and I hear him groan louder.

"Olivia." He calls my name once, twice, and three times.

"Let's go, cowboy!" I shout down the hall, and he comes storming down.

"Olivia." He stands there, and you can clearly see he's

aroused and it looks like it's going to break out. "You are not stepping foot out of that door unless you put something on."

"Really." I fold my arms over my chest. "Is that so?"

"What if you fall and your dress tears?" he asks. "Or what happens if there is an accident and they have to cut your dress off?" He stares at me and his eyes look like the deep end of the ocean. "What happens?"

I walk to him and stand in front of him. "What happens if I get so hot and bothered that I need you right then and there?" I ask him, knowing I'm testing him. I also know that I've never been this direct when it comes to sex. I was always shy and reserved, but something about Casey and I'm ready to say exactly what I want. "What if you have the sudden urge to push me against the wall?"

"Darlin'," he says in his Southern accent, and my knees go weak as his voice goes even lower. "If I want you that bad," he kisses right behind my ear, "I'll just rip them off." I shiver now.

"My panties are from France and they cost two hundred dollars each," I say, my chest heaving.

"I think I'm good for it." He winks at me now. "Now are we leaving or are you going to put on your two hundred dollar panties?"

"Relax, cowboy," I say, putting my hands on his chest and feeling his own heart beating as fast as mine. It's good to know that I'm not the only one struggling with this. "I'm perfectly covered."

"That's my girl," he says, and my stomach flutters again like a crashing wave. "Now the car is waiting."

"Lead the way." He grabs my hand, and the two of us walk out, my heels clicking on the marble floor. We walk through the lobby, and I can see the eyes turning to look at us. For the first time in my life, I don't know if they are looking at me or at him. I see the girls do a double take, and it makes me want to turn him around and claim him in front of them. Almost like "this is my man," but in reality, he's my man for the time being. We walk out, and the driver is standing next to the black Mercedes truck. He spots us and opens the door.

"Mr. and Mrs. Barnes," he says, and for the second time today, I don't correct them. I also don't think much of it. I get in, and the door closes behind me while Casey walks around the truck and gets in. He sits down and fixes his cuffs, and for the first time, I see that he's wearing black and gold cuff links.

He looks over at me, and I see his hair is falling a bit onto his forehead and my hand reaches out and pushes it away from his face. He reaches out and pulls me into his side, putting one arm around me. The driver gets into the car, and the whole ride there, I sit here next to him living in the moment. Not knowing that somewhere not too far away, someone just decided that the stakes have just been upped, and they will stop at nothing to get what they want from me.

Twenty-Four

CASEY

My heart pounds so hard in my chest I can't even talk. Walking into the bedroom and seeing her all dressed up knocked me on my ass. Beautiful isn't a good enough word to describe her. Now here I am mingling with her on my arm as she charms every person she meets. What makes her even more out of my league is that she doesn't even know that she has this aura about her.

"How long do we have to be here?" She smiles and leans over, and if you didn't know better, you would think she just told me a joke. When she takes another sip of her champagne, and she giggles, I have to just smile. Her cheeks are pink from the champagne.

"Not much longer," I say, taking a sip of the whiskey in my hand. We've been at this gala for the past two hours. My main goal was to go in and see if the company was viable and if I wanted to take it over.

"I'm starving," she says, still smiling, and I have to laugh. "Why are you laughing?"

I put my arm around her waist and bring her to me. "You just ate."

"I did not just eat. Did you see the portions?" She leans up, and I lean down to kiss her, something that I've been doing more and more tonight. "It's for birds."

"You've been eating my mother's portions," I joke with her, and she smiles.

"Casey." I hear my name and turn around to see the CEO coming straight for me. He's hitting sixty-five and just wants to travel the world. With no kids to pass the torch to, he opted to sell it. "I hope that you're having a great time."

"We are." I nod at him, and he looks over at Olivia and smiles, and I don't know why, but I want to throat punch him suddenly. "Aren't we, darlin'?"

"It's been a wonderful evening," she says, giving him her megawatt smile. "I was just telling Casey how great the team is and how in sync everyone is with each other." I almost laugh at her lying. "It would be a great company to work for."

He puts his hands in his pockets, and I could swear his chest is puffing out to please her. "If you are ever looking for a job ..."

She throws her head back and laughs. "Oh, no, I'll stick with designing." She looks at me and then at him. "But thank you for the offer."

His hand comes out now and he rubs her arm. "If you ever change your mind."

I want to snap at him that she won't. "Tonight was great," I say. "But we have another engagement to attend."

"Of course." He smiles. "Let me know if you have any questions." He nods and then smiles at Olivia. "It was great meeting you, Olivia," he says, putting out his hand.

"The pleasure was all mine," she says, shaking his hand, and if he pulls her in for a kiss on the cheek, I'm yanking her right back.

He doesn't, and when he walks away, she looks up at me and just laughs. "What?"

"If he touched you one more time, I was going to throat punch him," I say, and she laughs.

"Relax there, cowboy," she says, putting her hand on my chest. "I have eyes for one man and one man only."

"That so, darlin'?" I ask her, and I have the sudden need to throw her over my shoulder and take her back to the hotel and have my way with her.

"That is so, cowboy," she says and then she turns in my arms and wraps her arms around my shoulders. "Now can we please leave?"

"Let's go," I say, putting my drink down on an empty table on my way out. Her small hand is in mine as we walk out, and all eyes are all turned to us while we do it.

The driver is there waiting as soon as we walk out, and he opens the back door. I stand behind her to block her from all the visible eyes. Once the door is closed, I walk over and get into the car. This time, I unbutton my top button and loosen the tie. It's not often I have to dress up and when I do it, I hate every single thing about it. I thought I would love it, thought that it would make me feel more important, but I was wrong. It just made me want to go home faster.

"What do you want to eat?" I ask her and she looks over at me and her eyes twinkle. I shake my head and try to calm my throbbing cock. I had to spend most of the night with one hand in my pocket to hide my salute. "I mean, food."

"I mean, it's technically considered meat." She giggles. Leaning over, the driver takes a turn and she flies into my lap and she laughs.

"Darlin'," I say, trying to get her up and somehow she is straddling me, her dress riding even higher up her long legs. My hands go to her hips and she grabs my face and devours me. Her kisses are all tongue as she grinds herself into me. This isn't exactly how I thought it would happen. She lets go off my lips, and she bites her lower lip.

"You taste like whiskey," she whispers, and my eyes travel down to her chest that is rising and falling. "And Casey."

I laugh now as her hair falls in her face. "And what does Casey taste like?"

"Heaven," she says and slams her mouth down on mine again. I can't even say she's wrong, but I'm not the one who tastes like heaven. It's her; it's all her. My hands get lost in her hair. I get lost in her, so lost I don't notice the car stopping. It's only when I hear the driver clear his throat do I let go of her.

"We're here," I say softly, and I don't want to let her go.

"Promise me," she says in a whisper and I want to say that I'll promise her whatever she wants. "Promise me that we can finish this upstairs."

Her eyes looking at me, and I look at her lips swollen from my kisses and the little red marks around her mouth from my scruff. "How much did you have to drink?"

"Enough to give me the courage to ask you to finish upstairs," she says and then looks down. "Not enough to not remember every single moment."

"Are you sure?" I ask, holding my breath waiting for her to answer. Hoping like fuck she hasn't changed her mind.

"I haven't been sure about a lot of things in my life," she says, and her hands come to play with my tie. "But this?" She looks up at me. "I've never been surer of anything in my life."

"Thank fuck," I say, and in one move, I'm out the door and she's on her feet. Her hand remains tucked in mine as I walk as fast as I can to the private elevator. The sound of her heels click on the marble floor, and when I look over my shoulder, I see she is almost running to keep up with me. But not only that, she's stunning. Her smile is everything, and at the moment, I feel myself lost for her. I'm lost in her; I'm lost in everything that has to do with her and for the first time in my whole life I know what it feels like to love something so much it takes your breath away. I know what it feels like to want to protect something so much you'd give your life for it. For the first time in my whole life, my heart beats for another person, it beats along with hers.

When the elevator door closes behind her, I grab her and push her against the back of the elevator. "Casey," she whispers my name, and my mouth crashes down on hers. Her tongue tastes like champagne and whiskey. I grab her hips and push into her so she can feel how ready I am for her.

She moans into my mouth and arches her back. "Darlin'," I say as she lets go of my lips and moves down to my neck, biting me and then sucking in. The elevator pings, and I pick her up. Her dress hikes up so far that it's only covering her ass as she wraps her long legs around my waist. I walk to the door, one hand around her waist, the other looking for the fucking key. I finally get it open, and I shut the door with my foot and then press her frantically against the wall. Her tongue slides into my mouth as her fingers fuss with the tie around my neck. I leave her mouth and I move my mouth down to her neck biting her exactly where I know her heart beats. I suck it right after I bite it and her head hits the wall and I look up and see her eyes are closed.

"Stay with me," I say, and I move down to the top of her dress. I kiss her, and as I trail kisses down, I move her dress lower and lower until her nipple comes out, and I take the little pink pebble into my mouth. She moans out now as I press her deeper into the wall, my cock aligned right over her covered pussy.

"Casey," she says as her hands now go into my hair, and she holds on to me as I move from one nipple to the other. I let go of the other nipple, and I look down at her. Her dress is pushed down and her nipples are now out and glistening with the wetness of my mouth. Her back arches, and she tries to press into my cock as she moves her hips. "Casey," she says, and this time, her eyes flutter open and she looks at me. Her eyes are filled with lust, I peel her from the wall and walk into the living room.

"Where do you want me to devour you at?" I ask her, not giving a shit at this point. "Couch or bed?"

She looks at me. "Anywhere you want, cowboy." Her words are a whisper, and I think about taking her to the bedroom and laying her in the middle of the bed and feasting on her, but the need to feast on her makes me stop midway, and I place her on the couch. Her dress is hiked up, barely covering her. She watches my every move, and when I get on my knees and pull her legs forward until her ass is on the edge, she falls back a bit. But she gets up on her elbows as she watches me.

"I owe you," I say, and she just looks at me. "There is no way these panties are going to survive." I look at the lace panties, and in one move, I rip them off her. I'm face-to-face with her pussy, and I don't even take a minute to look at her. I can't; my mouth waters to taste her, and taste her I do. My mouth devours her pussy in one lick. One long, wet lick until I suck in her clit. Her moans are louder than before, and I look up at her as I bite down on her clit, and her legs close around my head. Her taste is addictive, and when she tries to sit up, I slip one of my fingers in her. Her arms give out. "Fuck," I hiss, turning to kiss her inner thigh and slip another finger into her. "I'm going to spend the rest of the night making you come over and over again." I don't even know if she can hear me between her pants and her moans. "Over and over again." I suck in her clit. "You're going to come." I move my fingers just a touch faster. "On my tongue." I slide my tongue in with my fingers, tasting her on my tongue again, and now it's my turn to moan. "On my fingers," I say, moving just a touch faster, and her hips move now while my tongue circles her clit, once and then twice. "And then," I say, my voice going soft and my fingers stopping. She groans, and her eyes open again this time only halfway. "With my cock," I say, looking into her eyes, and my thumb moves back and forth on her clit as I finger fuck her until she comes on my fingers.

Twenty-Five

OLIVIA

"With my cock." He looks into my eyes, and I get lost in him. All around me, his touch pushes me to the edge. From the minute he grabbed me in the elevator to the smooth way he got my dress down. His big rugged hands are no match for my flimsy lace panties and the second he touched them they disintegrated. I watch his blue eyes when his thumb starts to move back and forth on my clit as he finger fucks me until it becomes too much, and I come on his fingers. The minute I moan his name, his mouth devours me again. Dragging the orgasm out, my legs lock his head in until my body finally finishes.

I knew it would be out of this world. I knew that it would be nothing like before because I like him. I like him a lot, and this right here just pushed him into another category I wasn't ready for. But is anyone really ever ready for love? I sit up, and this time, it's me who grabs his face, and I kiss him. His tongue tastes like me and whiskey, and the more I taste, the more I want to taste more. My hands fall from his face to his chest, a chest I've fallen asleep on, a chest that I buried my face in when I cried. A chest that shivers under my touch now. My hands go down to his belt, and I slowly undo it while he tries to talk, but my mouth never leaves his. I slip open the button, and the sound of the zipper going down is drowned out by the moan that escapes him when my palm cups him. He's rock solid, and when my finger slips past the elastic band and touches the tip of his cock that is oozing precum, he lets go of my mouth.

"Darlin'." He says my name, and I look at him now.

"You had your fun, cowboy," I say, slipping down on my knees in front of him. I kiss under his chin and then kiss his neck right where I can feel his heart beating just as fast as mine. My tongue comes out and trails it to his shirt collar. "It's time to have mine," I say and bend to see his pants hanging off his hips, his black Calvins pushed down showing you just the tip of his cock. I lean forward and lick the tip, the saltiness hitting my tongue and making me take his head into my mouth. The need to bring him to his knees just as he did me takes over, and my hand comes out to cup his balls as I fist him. My fingers don't touch as I jack him off at the same time I move my head up and down.

"Darlin'," he says, pushing my hair away from my face, and I look up at him as he watches me take him in my mouth. "Fuck," he says as I gag on his cock when it hits the back of my throat. "Take me," he says softly. "All the way," he says, and I try again, but he's just so big I can't. "Slowly," he says but I don't want to go slow.

"No," I say, licking him from his balls to the top of his cock. "Not slow. Fast," I say, sucking him in again and then licking the other side of his cock now. "Fast, hard, and wet," I say.

"Is that what you want?" he asks, and my hand jerks him a couple of times.

"Yes," I say, and his eyes gloss over, and his cock throbs in my hands. So I lean down and take him again in my mouth, sucking him deep and then twirling my tongue around his head.

"Yes. I want you to sit on the couch, and I want to sink down on your cock," I say, and I shiver at the look on his face. He leans down and kisses me with his tongue while my hand jerks his cock, and I feel it getting bigger in my hand.

"I'm going," he starts to say, and I take him in my mouth again, and I suck him in as my name leaves his lips when he releases himself. I swallow him until he's done, and when I slip his cock out of my mouth, it is even harder than it was before.

"Darlin'." He pulls me up, kissing me while he does. He wraps one hand around my waist and almost as if I weigh as light as a feather, he stands up and now I wrap my legs around him.

"Playtime is over," he says, and I want to ask him what he means but instead I just sink into the kiss that he gives me. When we walk into the bedroom, he places me on the bed and then gets on his knees, taking off first one shoe and then the other. I reach out then and grab his hand, untying one cuff link and then the other. I slip his black jacket off his shoulders. My fingers loosen the silk tie around his neck and let it fall next to his jacket. The need to touch his chest is making my heart speed up. One button and then another and when I finally finish the last one, I lean in and kiss him right in the middle of his chest. I can feel his heart hammering in his chest, and with my two hands, I slip his shirt off. "My turn," he says, and I smile at him.

Leaning in, he slowly unzips the dress and pulls it over my head, and it lands in the pile of clothes. My bra follows along with his pants, boxers, shoes, and socks and the two of us are just letting our hands roam over each other's body. He leans down and grabs his pants and takes out his wallet and then the condoms that fall out of them on the floor in front of my feet. I laugh when the condom opens and I see it's six condoms. "Someone was thinking he was getting lucky."

He pushes the hair away from my face and cups my cheek. "Someone was hoping," he says and kisses me and leans me back on the bed coming down with me.

He kisses me until he leaves me breathless, and he cups my breast. I throw my leg over his hip, and my pussy comes into contact with his cock. It would take nothing for him to slide into me. It would take nothing for me to roll him over and sink down on him. "Casey," I say, and he just covers my mouth with his again.

He moves me effortlessly until I'm in the middle of the bed, and he's hovering over me. My legs spread for him when he gets on his knees and slowly rips a condom open with his teeth. Taking it out and placing it on his cock that I'm finally seeing all of, and there is a lot to see. I watch him sheath himself and I hold my breath when he takes his cock in his hand and rubs it down my slit.

"Watch me," he says to me, and my eyes never leave his hands as he rubs me again and then slowly puts the head at my entrance, and slowly, ever so slowly, his cock disappears inside me. Filling me and making me moan, I close my eyes and take in the feeling of him. My legs move up his hips now and lock behind his back as he falls forward on his elbows right beside my head.

"Olivia." He calls my name, and I open my eyes to look at him and when I'm looking deep into his eyes he comes out and enters me again this time in one deep thrust. "Olivia." He says my name over and over again between his pants and then kisses. Between his tongue slipping into my mouth or my breathing into his neck. The whole time my hands roam his arms and then his back. I can't get enough of him, the way he touches me and the way he slowly and deeply fucks me. I'm about to cry out but he covers my mouth with his again.

"Olivia." He says my name again and I'm so close to saying the three words I've never said to anyone before. Three words I thought I would never feel for another person.

I swallow the words, and the tears that are burning to come out, not because of sadness, but because I've never been this happy before in my life. I've never been this cherished with his mouth on my lips, my neck, my ear as he makes love to me. "Casey." I whisper his name when I'm close to the edge. "I'm almost there."

"I know, darlin'," he says, my clit igniting every single time he slams home as I try to pick up the friction. "Wet your finger," he says, and I stick my finger in my mouth. "Now play with your clit," he says and I move my hand down between us and I move my finger around it and he hisses out. "You got tighter," he says between clenched teeth. "Do it again," he says, and I play with my clit again, and again, my pussy is ready to let go. He leans in and licks my nipple and then he bites down the second he slams into me and I see stars. I come so hard I can't see anything except him.

I don't see anything except him, and when he throws his head back and plants himself as deep in as he can go, my name leaves his lips. "Olivia," he says and falls forward, his face buried in my neck. My limbs are now limp, but my legs stay locked around his waist, and my hand now hugging him. Our chest glues together as he rolls us to the side, never letting me go or coming out of me. "Olivia." He whispers my name again, and I wait for it. Wait for him to say something, wait to hear anything that he has to say. He doesn't say anything, he just lies there in my arms, and my hand curls up to play with his hair.

"I love you," I say softly to myself when I hear him snore softly beside me.

Twenty-Six

CASEY

"I love you." I can swear I hear it right before I close my eyes, but when I open them again, her eyes are closed, and her chest rises and falls.

I've just made love to her. There was no mistaking what we just did. The whole time I called her name, I told her I loved her silently to myself. The whole time in my arms, I cherished every single second we had, and I wasn't moving from this spot until she got up. I watch her as she lays her head on the pillow with my cock still buried in her. Only when she gets heavier in my arms do I let her go and slip out of her. I get off the bed as lightly as I can and walk to the bathroom to take off the condom and wash myself off. I toss the towel on the floor and put my hands on the counter and lean forward, letting my head hang. "How could you do it?" I look at myself in the mirror. "You went and fell in love with her." I don't even know when it happened. I don't even know how it happened, but just like that, I fell in love with her. Not just any love, the love that everyone tells you about. The all-consuming, you're never going to love another one like this kind of love.

I hang my head and walk out and see her on her side in the middle of the bed. My chest is closing in the closer I walk to the bed. Grabbing the blanket, I slide into bed with her, taking her in my arms.

"Casey," she mumbles. I just kiss her neck, and she slowly falls back asleep. I listen to her snore softly and bury herself deeper in my arms. I close my eyes for just a minute, but I fall asleep with her.

I feel her leave the bed, and I open one eye and watch her walk to the bathroom. I hear the water turn on and roll over to pick up the phone and order her favorite foods. When she comes back out of the bathroom, her hair is piled on her head, and she's wearing one of those plush white robes tied loosely.

"Did I wake you?" she asks. I see that she has washed off her makeup as she climbs back onto the bed. "I was quiet." She smiles at me and leans down and kisses me, and the kiss lingers after she slowly peels herself away. "Are you hungry?" she says, kissing my neck before sitting on the bed beside me.

"I just ordered a bunch of stuff," I say and see her eyes light up. "You didn't think I'd make you starve, did you?" I ask, and she rolls her eyes. "Besides, I plan on going a couple more rounds with you, so I need you to keep your strength up." She throws her head back, and the bathrobe falls open, and I lean over and take her nipple in my mouth. "Don't you dare start something you can't finish, Casey Barnes."

"Oh, I can finish," I say as I roll her over, and the sound of her laughter fills the room at the same time the knock on the door fills the room.

"Obviously, you can't." She pushes me off her and gets off the bed, about to walk out of the room.

"Where in the sam hill do you think you're going?" I hiss at her and grab her around the waist before she steps foot outside the room.

"I was going to answer the door." She looks back at me, shaking her head.

"Naked?" I ask, and she looks at me.

"I'm wearing a robe," she says, and I look at her grabbing my pants from the floor and slipping them on.

"You're in a robe naked underneath it." I glare at her. "If there is a gush of wind, then what?"

"A gush of wind?" she asks, folding her arms over her chest. "In the hallway?"

"You never know," I say. Turning to walk to the door, I stop to turn around. "Don't make me tie you up."

"Oh, you wish, cowboy," she says. There is another knock on the door, but she doesn't follow me. I open the door and see four people in the hallway with trays on their shoulders.

"Please come in, and you can put it on the dining room table," I tell them. They walk in, and I walk back to the bedroom where I see her sitting on the bed. "They are laying out the food."

"Can I come out yet?" she asks, and I shake my head.

"I'll call you when it's time," I say, walking to her and kissing her lips. "Don't come out before then."

"Oh, for the love of all the lard in the South," she says, and I laugh at her and walk out of the room and see the table all set. With fried chicken, chicken fried steak, grits and shrimp, collard greens, biscuits and gravy, cornbread, and so much more.

"Let me know if you need something else," the butler from this morning says, and I smile at him as he walks out of the room.

"Is it safe to come out?" she yells from the bedroom, and I laugh.

"You can come out now," I say, and she walks into the living room wearing my shirt that I had on a couple of hours ago. My cock immediately springs into action when I look at her, and then I look at the food, and I'm about to take her on the table when she points at me.

"You said I needed my strength so buckle it down, cowboy," she says, sitting down and grabbing a plate to help herself. "Do you know before last month, I had never eaten fried chicken?" she says, looking at me. I just watch her as she takes a bite and then looks at me. "Also, I didn't eat any carbs for ten years."

"At all?" I ask, grabbing my own plate and filling it up. She looks over at me and raises an eyebrow. "You aren't the only one who needs their strength." She laughs, and I lean over and softly kiss her lips.

"To be in the rodeo, did you have to be on a special diet?" she asks, and I shake my head.

"No, I guess I just needed to eat lots of protein and keep my cardio up," I say, taking a bite of the shrimp and grits and then looking over at her. "What about you?" She looks at me. "To walk the runway, did you?"

She puts her head back and laughs. "I've been on a diet since I was six and my mother thought I was getting a pouchy stomach," she says, and I grip my fork even harder. "I was allowed white fish, steamed veggies, and that is about all. My portions were also counted and no sugar. Not even on my birthday. I mean, once they tried to slip it to me at one of the pageants on the day of my birthday, but my mother threw it on the floor." She picks up her hands and does air quotes. "By accident."

I shake my head and make a mental note to buy her the biggest and sweetest cake that there can be for her next birthday. I try not to think that I might not be with her. Regardless, she's getting a huge cake. "My mother made all our cakes," I say, and she smiles, and her whole face lights up.

"I bet she did," she says as she takes a bite of the shrimp. The rest of the meal goes by with her stories of Kallie and her apartment and the only time she allowed ice cream into the house.

"I don't think I've ever been so full in my life," she says and leans back in the chair, and I laugh.

"You say that every single time you eat," I say, and then I hold out my hand for her and she gets up. "Let's go take a bath."

"You read my mind," she says and when I turn on the water and she puts bubbles in it, I try not to groan. Five minutes with her in the tub, and I'm forgetting that there are even bubbles when she sinks down on me. We both stop. "Oh my God," she says, but she doesn't move.

"Condom," I hiss out, my cock getting way too comfortable in her. "I've never went bareback," I say and try not to move.

"I've been tested," she says, and then looks down, embarrassed that she's been tested. "You know Dominic wasn't faithful, and after that, I just ..." I stop her from talking by kissing her until she forgets what she's saying. I put my hand on her hips and I move her up and down. "I have an IUD," she says right before I say I'm going to come, and we both come at the same time. I didn't even give a shit if she has anan IUD or not. I carry her out of the tub and we step into the shower to rinse off the bubbles.

When we finally collapse into bed, I take her in my arms and we both fall asleep in minutes. During the night, I take her two more times, and when I wake up and her ass is wiggling around, I do the only thing I can do. I pick her up by her hips and slide into her. She moans, awake.

"Casey," she mumbles, but she doesn't fight it. Instead, she fucks me back so hard I almost fall back, and when we both come, the both of us fall right back to sleep. But nothing could prepare me for waking up to my cock in her mouth. The heat all over my cock, and when I finally open my eyes, she smiles at me crawling over and sinking down on me.

"Time to ride the cowboy." She lifts herself up and then down again. My hands go up and cup her nipples, making her moan out and grind into me when I come down. Her hands go on my stomach, and then I lick my thumb and move it to her clit, knowing how much she likes it.

"Yes," she says and I sit up now, moving my back to the headboard, and she now grabs the headboard with both hands, and she fucks me like it's no one's business. "I'm so close," she pants out and I just watch her, one hand rolling her nipple between my fingers and the other playing with her clit.

"Right there," she moans out, and when I feel her pussy squeeze me tight, I lift my hips to meet her thrust. "Right there," she says and then she bends and bites my lower lip. "So close, cowboy." I lean forward now and bite her nipple down hard and then suck in, and it's what pushes her over the edge when she comes over my cock and she rides me the whole time. When I know she's done I grab her around her waist and flip her over, and she spreads her legs. I put both legs over my shoulders as I fuck her now harder than before. The sounds of our skin slapping together fills the room until I plant myself balls deep and come yet again.

Twenty-Seven

OLIVIA

He gets out of the shower before me, leaving me to rinse the shampoo that I put in my hair five minutes ago. I slipped into the shower after the last round of sex we had on the dining room table. I had maple syrup in my hair and in other places, I didn't think it would get better after the second and even the third time, but every single time is better than the last time.

"We have to be in the office in forty-five minutes," he says from beside the sink. I rub the mirrored door and see him standing there with a towel around his hips. Even though I've touched, kissed, and licked almost every single part of him, I still get tingles. "You think you can be ready?"

"Are you going to give me a chance to get dressed?" He watches me in the mirror, and he just smiles at me. "As long as you're not peeling off my clothes, I think I can be ready in thirty."

He just laughs. "I bet you that you won't be ready." He looks over at me, and I just look at him.

"What are we betting?" I ask him, and my competitiveness takes over.

"If I win, I get to fuck you the way I want to." He smirks, and I tilt my head. "And if you win, I eat you for an hour."

"I don't know how I would lose in any way," I say, and he shakes his head and comes to the shower door opening.

His eyes are so dark that if I didn't know any better, I would think they were black. "Fucking you how I want is hours and hours, and you not coming until I want you to."

"Again." I turn the water off. "How am I losing in all of this?"

"Are we bettin', darlin'?" he says in the most Southern accent I've ever heard.

"Oh, we're bettin', cowboy," I say and grab a towel wrapping my hair up in it. "The question is do I make you win or do I lose because either way," my hand slips the towel off him and I see his cock is ready to play, "I end up with this." Grabbing his cock in my hand. "Or your mouth and I can't decide which one I like better." I lean up and kiss him under his chin but not before squeezing him in my hand and then turning to walk away.

"That's the best ass I've seen," he says, and I look back over my shoulder and see the twinkle in his eye. "I'm going to have fun making it mine."

"Again, cowboy, I don't know how I could ever lose." I wink at him and walk over to my closet after my shower. I grab the pink skirt and white halter top from the closet, slipping another pair of lace silk panties on and my matching lace demi bra. It leaves me ten minutes to do my hair since I've learned way back when that my hair is naturally beach ready. I apply just a touch of mascara, and I slip my skirt on and zip it on the side, tying the long pink sash in the front. I slip the white shirt on and tuck it in. Grabbing my pink suede Louboutins, I slip on some bangles and then my gold Rolex watch that I haven't put on in over two months.

"Okay, cowboy," I say, walking out of the room and stopping in my tracks when he comes out of his room. He's dressed in another suit; this time, it's blue with light white pinstripes, and he's tying a gray silk tie. His hair looks like he just brushed it back with his hand, and his scruff is a bit longer today, but what makes me stop is the way he dominates the suit. "Looks like you lose." I try not to let him in the suit get to me, or at least I try not to let him know how much it gets to me.

He shakes his head and checks his Rolex watch. "Looks like I did."

"Well, then." Walking to him, I can smell his aftershave, and I can't decide if I love Casey with the woodsy smell or Casey with the musky smell. There is that word again love. "I guess I do lose."

"That's right, sucker," I say, and he throws his head back laughing, one of his arms coming out and bringing me close to him. His hand is resting on my ass. "I can't decide," I say softly to him, fixing his tie. "Which Casey I like more."

"Always go with the cowboy." He leans forward and kisses me. "That's the real Casey."

His phone rings before I can answer him, and he looks down. "We're on our way there right now." I don't know who is on the phone, but his face goes from a smile to a stone face. "I want security in place." He looks at me. "Set up the safe house just in case." He disconnects and then he looks at me.

"We need to go right now," he says, and the tone in his voice shows me he's not joking.

"What happened?" I ask and follow him quickly out of the room and to the elevator. He looks around the lobby the whole time until we are safe in the car and my heart is pounding so fast I don't think I will be able to hear him talking. "You're scaring me," I say and my mouth goes dry.

"Darlin'," he says and grabs my face in his hand, making it

so much worse. "I'll explain everything once we get to the office, and I have all the information." He tries to appease me by kissing me lightly on the lips, but it doesn't help. My whole body goes cold, and I don't even notice that I'm shaking until he takes off his jacket and puts it around my shoulders. When we get to the office, he almost shields me, bringing me into the office. We walk past the receptionist and go straight to the room I was in yesterday.

When we walk in, Derek looks up, and he takes off his headset that he's wearing, and the room is darker than it was yesterday. "Turn on the light," Derek says to Casey, and the lights come on lightly.

Casey walks over to the side and grabs a chair and rolls it to me. "Sit," he orders. I sit down, and I just look at him and then at Derek.

"One of you is going to have to tell me what in the sam hill is going on right now," I say, and Derek looks at Casey and he just nods his head, but he holds his hand up, getting in front of me and squatting down.

"I want you to know that nothing is going to happen to you," he says, kissing my hands in his. The tears come to my eyes before I can even fight them off.

"Casey," I say his name, and he hangs his head in defeat.

"Derek," he says, "you can start."

"Okay," Derek says, and I look down at Casey who doesn't move from in front of me, nor does he let my hands go. "I will go step by step."

"That works." I take one hand away from Casey and wipe my cheek.

"This is your cell phone," Derek says, and one of the television screens shows me my telephone screen. The background of the Eiffel Tower fills the screen with my applications all around it.

"As you can see you have your basic applications," he says. "Your photos, settings, maps, camera, Instagram, and Facebook." He gets up from his chair and walks over to the screen. "Looks normal, right?"

"Yes," I say, not understanding why my phone is such a big deal.

"But then you have this little folder here," he says, pointing at one that is written NEWS under it.

"I put all the news under one," I say, and he looks over at me.

"TMZ and People is not news," Derek says, and I just roll my eyes. "But anyway, there was another application in there that was marked INTL." He shows me, and I look at it and I just shrug.

"I don't know what that is," I say. "I mean, I saw it, but I never opened it. I assumed it came with the phone."

"It didn't," Derek says and clicks on the app, and you can see the cursor blink. "Look at this. I'm going to text you," he says, taking his phone and texting me. The text comes through, but it also registers in the INTL. "This is how he tracked you and everything that you typed. He also had your locations on it."

"What a douche," I say and then look at Casey. "This isn't as bad as I thought."

"There is more," Derek says. "So not only was he tracking you," he says, "but I think he buried something either on your phone or on your iPad or on your computer."

"I don't have an iPad," I tell them. "My computer." Looking at both of them. "There is nothing on my computer. I only use it for work."

"Did you ever have it around Dominic?" Derek asks, and I nod. "Where is the computer now?"

"At the hotel," I tell them, and then I look at Casey.

"I'm going to have someone go there right now and get it,"

Casey says, and Derek nods, taking out his phone and texting someone and then putting his phone away.

"Okay, so now that we have one part settled," Derek says. "Or at least we can checkbox one, it might be the reason everyone is so determined to get to you."

"Who is trying to get to me?" I ask him and then answer for him. "Is it Dominic? I mean, how can he? He's locked up."

"Yes, but his associates aren't," Derek points out. "He's in jail, but whoever he is working with isn't."

"Okay, this is going above and beyond," I say, getting angry now. "I don't know anything about his associates. I don't know who he worked for, and I don't know who worked for him. I know nothing."

"But they don't know that," Casey says. "For all they know, you know everything, and you are hiding it for him."

"Well, who are these people? I could maybe call them and tell them that I know nothing." I start to get angry. "I mean, do I take out a billboard in Times Square? Do I grant CNN an interview? What the hell can I do?"

"There was a couple of visitors that Dominic got a couple of weeks ago," Derek starts to say. "I got a copy of their conversation, and it's all in code." My eyebrows go together. "They talked about the sun in India and then the water in Bora Bora."

"Again. No idea," I say, and he looks down and then up at me, and just from his look, I know that shit is going to get worse.

"He got to use the phone yesterday," he says. "He called the same man who visited him in prison." I wait for it. "He wants to wipe the slate clean."

"That's good, right?" I ask. "Means he's ready to 'fess up."

"Not exactly," Derek says. "Someone put a price on your head." I look at him and then at Casey, not sure I understand.

"What does that mean?" I ask, waiting for someone to answer me.

Casey is the one who answers me. "It means there is a contract out there to end your life."

Twenty-Eight

CASEY

I watch her face when I say what Derek told me not even thirty minutes ago. I watch and see the words sink into her, and then I watch her crumple in front of me.

"Why?" she asks, lips quivering while she does it.

"We have the FBI on their way here," Derek says, "and when I get the computer, I can see if something is on there. But bottom line. You have something that they need and now they are done waiting for it."

She shakes her head and gets angry. "I don't fucking have anything."

"I know you don't," I say, and I don't say that my parents' house is under surveillance; I don't say that Jacob and Kallie are staying at my house because they are set up with cameras, and that Jacob feels safer having eyes all around him. I don't say that my mother is beside herself with worry for her and wants her home because I'm afraid that she won't go. Instead of going where she is going to be safe, she'll run away from it to make sure the people she cares about are safe.

"All of this." She gets up now and starts to pace. "All of this has nothing to do with me. Not one thing."

"I know it doesn't," I say, getting up now. "But ..." I'm about to say something when Derek gets a ping on his phone.

"He's using the phone," he says, and then I look at him as he presses the button, and you hear ringing.

Someone answers the phone, and the operator comes on, *"There is an inmate from a correctional facility."* You hear the sound of someone pressing the button.

"Hey," Dominic says, and I look over at Olivia who stands there. "What's new?"

"Nothing. I'm in Atlanta," the guy on the other line says. "It's hot as balls, but a lot better than the fucking South."

"Did you clean up the place?" Dominic asks, and I want to spend five minutes with him and wring his fucking neck. I actually need two minutes alone with him, just two minutes.

"I tried," he says. "Can't get close enough."

"You need to just erase it all," Dominic says.

"She's kept under lock and key. She has that cowboy trailing her like her pussy is the missing link."

"Trust me, I've been in that pussy. It's cold as ice." I want to tell Derek to shut it down.

"Maybe if your dick stayed hard longer than thirty-five seconds, my pussy would be warmer, you piece of monkey shit!" Olivia shouts. I can see something in her change, and she looks over at me. "I want to do whatever I need to do to make sure that he dies." She folds her hands. "I mean, I don't want anyone to kill him, but I want to." She tries to think of the words.

"You want to bury him?" Derek says with a smirk, and Dominic's voice cuts in.

"Just get what we need, or else I'll be the next one hanging in my cell," he says, and I look over at Derek, and he nods.

"It should be taken care of tonight," he says. "Call me back tomorrow."

"Yeah," Dominic says and hangs up.

"Who was that?" I ask Derek, and he goes to the computer and types something, and the man's face comes onto the screen.

"Meet Peter Bostrov," Derek says. "Also known as ex-KGB."

"What is that?" Olivia asks from beside me, and the need to hold her hand rips through me.

"It's ex-military for Russia." I look at her.

"Oh, perfect. I have an ex-Russian spy trying to kill me. God, and I thought today would be a good day."

"It started out good," I say, and she smiles at me.

"It might end with me dead." She tries to joke, but it gets to me. "I mean, not literally."

"This is the man who broke into the house, and who was setting traps on your property," Derek says, and now it's my turn to look at him. "What I didn't tell you until I got confirmation was that he was setting up traps at your house. He was going to light it all up."

"Oh my God," Olivia says from beside me, and whatever strength and fierceness she had ten minutes ago is gone. "Your parents." She looks over, and the tears are running down her face. "And the horses and your house." The sobs rip through her, and she folds over. I grab her now in my arms.

"I'll give you guys a minute," Derek says. After he walks out of the room, I hold her face in my hands.

"Look at me, darlin'," I say. She looks at me, and her eyes are so bright I could get lost in them. "Everyone is fine," I say. "We got all of the traps out and took care of it. I also have people at the farm locking it down so no one is going to get hurt."

"But ..." She starts to say and puts her hands on my hips.

"But nothing," I say. "Now I want to warn you. Today is going to suck," I say. "It's going to be the suckiest day you've ever had. But ...?"

"It might be my last," she says, and I want to say it can't be her last because we are just beginning.

"Can't be your last." I kiss her. "I still have a bet that needs to be collected." She smiles now, and then there is a knock on the door, and Derek comes back in.

"Feds are here," he says, and I look at her.

"I need to wash my face," she says, and I nod and show her where the bathroom is. Then I walk back into the room and see Derek standing there with the computer in his hand.

"Is she okay?" he asks, and I shake my head.

"You going to say how you feel before all this?" I look over at him. "I never thought I would see the day that badass cowboy Casey Barnes falls in love and breaks his whole I'm never getting married bullshit."

"It's not bullshit," I say and then turn back to look at the closed door. "I'm not getting married."

"Then you're not as smart as I thought you were." He plugs the computer in.

"What the fuck does that mean?" I ask.

"It means that if you don't marry her, someone else will, and then what?" he says, knowing that it's going to burn me. "You going to watch her come visit Kallie with her husband and kids and not kick yourself for letting her go."

"She ..." I start to say, and then the door opens, so I stop, and I look over at her. "You ready?"

"No," she answers honestly. "But there is no time like the present."

"Let's do this," Derek says, and he walks out of the room. I grab Olivia's hand and walk with her into the conference room.

We walk in, and I scan the room and hear Olivia say from beside me. "Isn't he the butler?" She points at the butler from the hotel.

CHAPTER TWENTY-EIGHT

"Special Agent Duchene." He says his name. "Thank you for not being a diva."

"Did you know?" She looks at me, and I answer her honestly.

"I did. They got to me right before we took off," I say. "Shall we sit?" I motion for her to sit down, and I sit down next to her. There are five guys around the table all dressed in suits, all with the USA flag pinned to their lapel.

"Olivia," one of them says. "My name is Special Agent Robinson, and we've been watching you for the past six months."

"What?" she says, and even I'm surprised they would say that.

"Dominic Albano is mixed up with the wrong type of people. He doesn't know it, but his time is almost out, and the people who he owes are tired of waiting for him."

"I don't know what that means," she says, looking at them. Her hands shake, but I take one of them in my hand, and I have to hold it in both of my hands because it's cold as ice.

"It means that he owes the mob a lot of money. More money than his ass can cash," one of the other agents says.

"Is that who is after me? The mob?" she asks, and they all shake their head.

"They want nothing to do with you," Special Agent Duchene says. "They told him that he made the deal with them, not you."

"I don't know what they want." She looks around the table. "Honestly, I don't. I have thought and thought, and there is nothing that he told me, nothing that he gave me, nothing."

"I just got her computer," Derek says. "It may take me an hour, but I can see if there is anything in there."

"Please do," one of the agent says, and Derek gets up and then looks at Olivia.

"Can you come with me so you can see if anything looks unfamiliar to you?" he asks. Olivia gets up and walks out with them, and only when she's out of earshot do I look back at the table.

"Now that she isn't here, what aren't you telling her?" I ask them. "And it's safe to say that even if you don't want me to know, we all know that I can find out."

They share a look, and then Special Agent Duchene takes the lead. "We have to send her in," he says. "She has to go see Dominic and try to trick him into spilling his guts."

"No fucking way," I say, shaking my head. "No fucking way in hell is she going in there."

"It's the only way to get rid of him," the other guy says. "We have the evidence but having him admit it is something else."

"If she goes in, I go in with her," I tell them.

"This has nothing to do with you," one of them says, and I laugh.

"This has everything to do with me." I stare at them. "Dominic put me in this fight when he sent people to my motherfucking house and had one point a gun at me. He put me in the middle of this when he tried to blow up my fucking farm."

"You aren't trained," one of them starts to say, and I laugh.

"I trained with the SEALS for six months for fun," I tell them. "I'm going in." They don't say anything when Derek comes barging into the room.

"Holy fuck, you guys," he says, his eyes big and wide. "I think I found what he's looking for."

Twenty-Nine

OLIVIA

I watch the screen with all the green numbers, and I wonder what the hell just made Derek jump out of his chair and run out to get Casey. When I walked into the room, and he opened the computer, I tried not to groan when he made fun of my screensaver. Then he showed me what looked like a little icon on another page that I didn't even know how to get to. When he clicked on it, all these numbers poured onto the screen.

The door opens, and Casey comes running in first, followed by Derek and the agents behind them. He walks over to the screen and sees the numbers. "They are routing codes."

"That is what I'm thinking also," Derek says, sitting down and typing other things.

"This looks like the number of an account," Casey says, and I'm in awe at how he just looked at it and knew what it was. Making me ask myself why he hides this side of him. "This is a Cayman account number."

"On it." Derek types it in, and then I hear him say, "Oh my God."

"What?" I ask him now, my heart pumping. I don't know how much more I can handle today.

"Did you ever go to the Cayman Islands?" he asks, and I shake my head. "Are you sure?"

"I think I know where I visited and when," I say and look at Casey. I point at the computers in front of him. "You have something on there that can track my passport. You can check."

"Well, according to the documents," Derek says, "you own twenty offshore accounts."

Yup, that is the straw that broke the camel's back for Casey, and he roars out. "I don't give a shit that you are Special Forces. I don't give a fuck that what I say can bite me in the ass. If I find this guy, he isn't coming out alive." I gasp, walking over to him. Now it's me taking his face in my hands and having him look at me.

"You cannot let him win," I say, then I look over at the agents. "He's from the country. He gets riled up easily."

Derek laughs. "Yeah, let's blame the country for him." He shakes his head. "According to this, you also"—he types more—"have accounts in the Bahamas, Switzerland, and Belize."

"I have to sit down," I say to Casey. He brings me to the chair, sits down, and then pulls me onto his lap.

"I'm not letting you go," he says, and if we didn't have a room full of people, I'd show him how much I'm not letting him go either.

"How much money are in those accounts?" one of the agents asks, and Casey speaks up.

"You'll find that out after my lawyer drafts certain documents saying that this doesn't touch Olivia, and that anything you find is not on her."

"It's not on me because I didn't do it," I tell the room. "Can you check the signatures?"

"Those can be doctored," Derek says. "What can't be doctored is the video surveillance."

"Those are only kept for ninety days," one of the agent says. "Some keep them for seven years, but the majority of them don't."

"There has to be some way," I start to say, and I don't miss the look that everyone gives each other. "What?"

"The only way for that to happen is for you to confront Dominic face-to-face," Special Agent Duchene says.

"Oh, I would love to do that," I tell them. "But he's in jail."

"We can get you in," an agent says. "You'd be between the glass, and the chances that he will even admit to anything is slim to none."

"Not if she tells him that she is going to spend it all," Derek says, leaning in his chair. "Hear me out. He owes the mob a fuck ton. My guess is that he was banking on getting the money from the offshore accounts in order to get them off his back. What if she goes in there and says that she spent it all? I don't know about you, but that would make me crazy as fuck."

"She's not going in," Casey says, and I look at him.

"It's the only way," I say. "It's the only way I can be free of him."

"There has to be another way," he says.

"Yeah, there is, and that is with me dead." I try to joke. "Which is not the option I choose." I look over at the agents. "Let's do it."

"We will work on it right away," one agent says and walks out of the room to talk on his phone.

"What about the guy who is waiting to take me out?" I ask the rest of them.

"Right now." One of the agents laughs. "He's being arrested for breaking into your hotel room."

Then he looks at Casey. "Thanks for the tip."

"How did you know?" I ask him, and he looks at me.

"When he called Dominic, Derek kind of put a bug on his line, and we tracked the towers," he says, and I look at him with my mouth hanging open.

I lean in and whisper, "You sound so sexy right now." The agent comes back into the room.

"We have a plane ready in fifteen. We should be in LA in five hours, which will be three p.m. LA time," the agent says.

"Perfect," Casey says, and I get up. "She doesn't go in that place until the document is signed." He looks over at Derek.

"Should be in your email in an hour tops," Derek says, and then he smiles at me. "I'll be watching the whole time."

"How?" one of the agents ask.

"That's not really your concern," Casey tells him, and then we turn to walk out of the room. Casey holds my hand in the elevator, and when we get down to the parking garage, you would think that the president is in town with the black trucks waiting.

I get into one of the trucks with Casey right behind me, and two agents get into the front. "Are you okay?" He leans over and whispers to me, and I look at him, and I answer him honestly.

"I'm not sure." I look at him and then to the front where the agents are sitting. "I only hope for one thing." Turning to look at Casey, I say, "That after tonight, it will all be over."

"It will be," he says, putting his arm over me and pulling me to him. I feel his warmth run through me as I look out the window at the passing scenery. We arrive at the same airport that we arrived at, but this time, the plane is just a touch bigger. I sit in one of the chairs with Casey right next to me, and the four special agents sit together in front of us. I look out the window as we take off down the runway. I close my eyes, hoping like fuck that this is it. That this is going to be the end of this nightmare, and I can finally get on with my life.

"Excuse me, Ms. Young." I open my eyes and see Special Agent Duchene. "I was wondering if we can ask you a couple of questions and also explain to you how this is going to work."

"She's not answering anything without a lawyer here," Casey says from beside me, and I look over. He sits there in his chair, his fingers flying over his laptop that he must have taken out when we took off. "But lucky for you guys, I have my lawyer on standby." He puts his laptop on the table in front of us and the screen shows a lawyer. "Olivia, meet your lawyer, David Stern."

He watches me, and he nods at me. "Pleasure to meet you, Olivia."

"I guess it's a pleasure to meet you also," I say, and then I look at Casey, who smiles at me. It's funny how I never had someone actually take care of me. I would have to take care of myself. Make sure I was okay all the time, make sure that I got to places on time. The only time my mother really cared was when it was a red carpet event.

"So we are going to ask you just a couple of questions," the other agent asks. "When did you know that he was stealing money?"

"Gentlemen," David says, laughing. "She's not answering that question."

I lean over and whisper to Casey. "But I have nothing to hide." He looks at me and makes sure that the agents can't read his lips when he whispers back to me.

"They are trying to trap you," he says. "Trust me, you don't answer anything that David tells you not to."

"Okay," I say to him, and he kisses me. I turn to look at the agents. "I guess I'm not answering that question."

"Did you know anyone with the name Sorrento?" the

agent asks, and I just wait for the rest of the question, but instead, he opens a folder and takes out a picture and hands it to me. I grab it and look down at it.

"No." I hand it back to him.

"Are you sure?" he asks, and I laugh.

"Do you think I want to protect Dominic?" I ask him, and then look at all of the agents. "Do you think after everything he's done to me, I want to lie for him?" I laugh now bitterly. "This man did nothing for me, nothing. Instead, he threw me into a cage with wolves ready to pounce on me. So to answer any of your questions, and just so we're clear. I don't know who that man is."

The agents share a look, and then one leans forward. "We are going to want you to wear a wire when you go see him."

"Everything will be recorded anyway through the phone, but just in case, we want to make sure."

"Fine," I say to them, and then I ask them. "Will I be face-to-face with him?" My heart starts to speed up just a touch at the thought of seeing him after everything.

"No," Casey says from beside me. "It's through a bullet-proof glass with guards on his side." He looks at the agents. "That's not even up for a debate, or there is no fucking way she goes in there."

"We wouldn't put her in danger," Special Agent Duchene says. "We land in an hour and a half."

"Thank you, gentlemen. I have sent over the document for you to sign on behalf of my client. She doesn't walk in there unless the terms are agreed on," David says and then hangs up.

I look over at Casey. "Can we go straight home after this?" I ask him, and I'm about to kick myself when I say home. "I mean, can we can go back to the farm after this?"

He looks at me. "We'll go home after this."

I look out the window, and for the rest of the flight, I try to calm myself down. But when I step foot in Los Angeles, my feet itch to run back on the plane and leave. I look down the whole time, hoping no one sees the tears in my eyes. It's then I finally realize I can never come back here. I don't have time to overthink it because when I finally sit in the car, Casey takes my hand in his and brings it to his lips. "The plane is on standby whenever we are ready." I don't answer him. I can't, there is so much going through me right now I have no idea what I would say. So instead, I just nod.

When the car comes to a stop, my stomach lurches, and my hands get clammy. When I step foot out of the car, the sun's heat doesn't help the coldness that now runs through me. I walk with my hand in Casey's as we walk toward a gate that opens when the six of us stand there. The clinking of chain links makes me look up to see the tower with guards in it, and then my eyes find the barbed wire on the top of it. We walk in, and each of us sign in. We walk through the metal detector. Everything around me happens with a blur. We walk into an office, and a female officer is there, and she hooks me up to a wire that is taped under my shirt.

"He's ready for you," the agent says, and I try not to vomit all over the place. The nerves are real. "We need him to say that he put that money there." He goes on to say other things, but the beating of my heart blocks out his voice.

Casey looks like he's going to jump out of his skin. "If at any time you want out, I want you to get up and walk out," he says, his eyes clouded over. "Do you hear me, darlin'?"

I nod at him and turn to walk out of the room. I don't say anything as we walk down the concrete hallway, and the door at the end opens, and I walk into the dimly lit room. Eight chairs in a row face the glass separator with a wall on each side to give you some semblance of privacy.

"Number two," the guard says to me, and I walk down and sit on the metal chair and wait. The seconds feel like hours. The minutes like years and then I hear the click of the metal door on the other side, and it opens. I see Dominic before he sees me. His hands and feet are shackled together, the guard pointing down. He smirks at him and walks down, and the minute he sees me, his face goes white. "What's the matter, Dominic? Wasn't expecting me?" I ask him, hoping that he is just as nervous as I am to see me.

"Olivia." He says my name, sitting down in the chair in front of me. "Baby face." I loathe his voice, and the nickname makes my skin crawl. "I'm so happy you came to see me."

"Are you?" I ask him and laugh now. "Isn't that funny? I somehow got another message." He looks at me, and I see the change in him when he knows that I'm fucking with him.

"You look good for someone who has a concussion." He sneers. "Too good."

"I have to say," I say, shaking my head. "I spent the whole month going over everything in my head." I tap my fingers on the table in front of me. "Trying to think what is it that they wanted from me."

"Trust me," he starts to say, "there is nothing that you have that I want. I've been there, and I've done that. Obviously, as you saw, you didn't really do it for me."

"Really?" I say, now pissed. "There is nothing that you want from me?" I lean back and fold my hands, and then I think of the wire and uncross my arms. "I would imagine that you would definitely want me to get some of the money out." If he wasn't white before, he is now. Whatever color he had left is now gone from his face. "Oh, you see." I lean in. "I know about the money."

"I don't know what you're talking about," he says and looks around. "No idea what you are talking about."

"Well, then it's a good thing because I spent some of it." He glares at me, and I see that his body's starting to shake. "Okay, fine, you got me. I spent a lot of it. I always wanted to have a house in the Bahamas. Then I got a beautiful house on the beach in Belize." I look up at the ceiling. "I then spent ..."

He slams his hand on the table in front of him. "Enough, you fucking bitch. " He leans in, and if I was in front of him without the mirror, I would assume he would lunge for me, but I also have to know that I would have fought back.

"NO!" I shout out now. "It's not enough. It will never be enough. What you did was something that a spineless coward would do, and let's be honest. I shouldn't have expected anything else." I start to stand. "Goodbye, Dominic, I'll think of you every single time I spend a penny of that money."

"What?" he says nervously. "Olivia, wait." I turn around. "Please," he begs now. "You don't understand. If you don't give me the money, they are going to ..." He stops talking when I turn back around.

"Funny, I thought you had no idea what I was talking about? Now all of a sudden, you know." I shake my head. "You worthless piece of shit. You put those fucking accounts in my name without me even knowing."

"Listen to me, Olivia. I didn't mean to get you involved in all of this. But," he says, looking at me, "I had no choice."

"We all have choices," I say and walk back to him "Don't we, Dominic?" I put my hands on the table in front of me. "Just like the choice you made to put a bounty on my head." I refuse to show him how scared I am. I refuse to show him one more tear.

"I'm sorry," he now says. "But I need you to get me that money," he starts to say. "I never wanted to hurt you."

I shake my head. "The only thing you are sorry for is that you didn't win."

"I need that money!" He starts to yell. "Give me back my money!"

I look at him one last time, and I don't even say goodbye to him. I walk away, and then I hear him banging on the glass.

"I'll fucking kill you myself, you fucking bitch!" he shouts. "I will fucking end you." I put my hand to my stomach, and I see it's shaking. The guard opens the door, and once I'm out of the room, I bend over and vomit in the trash bin that is in the corner.

Thirty

CASEY

The minute she turns and walks away from him, I'm out that fucking door, making sure I'm there for her. I find her right before she throws up in the trash can in the corner.

I waited for her the whole time, pacing the small fucking room. The whole time, listening to the conversation. She sits there with all the grace in the world, showing him that he isn't in charge of her. Showing him that he doesn't have anything on her. Showing him that she is a motherfucking boss, exactly as I knew she would. She didn't waver, she didn't shake, she didn't shed a tear. She did none of that and I was so proud of her. But now seeing her throw up and shaking I want to bust into that room and end his life myself. "Darlin'."

I rub her back and then hold out a handkerchief for her. She puts it to her mouth and then looks up at me. Tears well in her eyes. "I hope it was okay."

"It was perfect." I take her face in mine. "You were perfect." I take her in my arms, and she wraps her arms around my waist.

"Olivia." I hear Agent Duchene call her name. "You got it." He smiled at her.

191

"Get the wire off her," I say. "My car is waiting and so is my plane." He nods, and they take her into the room, and the lady comes over and unclips all the wires from her.

When we walk out of the room the detectives are there. "If we need anything, where can we reach you?"

"She's going to be with me," I tell them. "You can reach her through me or through David," I tell them. "You have my number and his also." I put my arm around her and turn her around to walk out of the prison. I don't even bother looking back, and when we get into the car, she puts her head back and closes her eyes.

"Are you okay?" She opens her eyes and shakes her head.

"No." She blinks away tears. "I'm not okay. Nothing about this and today was okay and that sucks." I'm about to say something. "It started so well and then this." She turns to look out of the window, and I don't say anything else. I watch her, and when we get on the plane, she takes a bite of her food and then goes to lie down. I sit next to her while she lies down on the couch that they turned into a bed. I watch her the whole time, my own thoughts going all over the place and when the wheels touch down, I pick her up and carry her to the truck. She mumbles and wakes up for just a minute and looks around.

"Did we land?" she asks, and I push the hair away from her face.

"We did," I say. "Rest." She puts her head back and closes her eyes. I make my way to the house and when we get there, I see the lights are off and I know that Jacob and Kallie left this afternoon when they arrested Dominic's guy. I pull up and as delicately as I can I take her out of the truck. She is dead to the world, everything that she went through the past couple of months finally came full circle today. I tuck her into the bed, after I take off her shoes. I undress myself and grab a bottle of water going to the bed. The whole night I don't sleep, instead I watch her, making sure she is okay.

When the sun comes up, she stirs next to me and she blinks open her eyes. "What time is it?" she mumbles, stretching out beside me.

"Six," I say, just watching her and taking in everything thing about her.

"I guess I was really tired." She laughs and then looks over at me. Her eyes are lighter this morning.

"Are you hungry?" I get out of the bed now, afraid to touch her, knowing that one touch would not be enough, knowing that with her one touch is never enough.

"I am just a bit," she says, watching me grab a T-shirt and put it on. "Do you have to get going?"

"I have an appointment with Beau in an hour," I say, avoiding her eyes. "I'll go start the coffee." Turning to walk out of the room my chest is so tight, it's surprising I can breathe. I start the coffee and stand here, watching it drip. My head is telling me that it's better this way, my heart yearning to go back into the room and declare my love for her.

The soft knock on the back door makes me look up, and I see Kallie standing there with Jacob behind her. I walk over, unlocking it, and the door opens.

"Hey," Kallie says to me. "Is she up?" She looks over at the hallway, and I nod my head. She starts to walk down to the spare room, but I stop her.

"She's in my bed," I say, and when she turns to say something, I put my hand up, and she must see something else because she doesn't say a word. She says nothing. All she does is turn and walk to my bedroom.

I wait until she is out of sight before I turn to Jacob, and he just looks at me. "Did you get the news?"

"I did," he says. "I got a call from the detective early this morning. He was hanging in his cell."

I shake my head. I want to say I'm surprised, but nothing about Dominic surprises me especially the way he took the coward's way out. "Derek sent me an email at three forty-seven. He was revived on the scene but died on the way to the hospital." I shake my head. "Fucking coward."

"He knew the end was coming for him," Jacob says, and I walk back over to the coffee machine and pour myself a cup. "It was only a matter of time. Does she know?"

I shake my head and take a long gulp of the hot coffee. "No, I haven't said anything to her."

"Do you want me to do it?" he asks, and I shake my head.

"No, I'll do it when I come back," I say, putting down my coffee.

"Where the hell are you going?" he asks, his eyes almost glaring.

"I have to meet Beau in thirty minutes." I avoid his eyes this time.

"You really going to leave her?" he asks. I don't know if he's asking about now or in general. Either way, I don't have an answer for him. I have nothing.

"She's with Kallie. She'll be fine." I finish the coffee, ignoring the burning in my stomach. "Let her know I'm going to be back." I turn to walk out of the room.

"Don't do this," he whispers, and I turn around. "She needs." I stop him before he says the words I don't want to hear.

"She has everything she needs here. I'll be back," I say, walking to the front door and slipping on my Nike's. I grab my keys and my baseball hat and walk out of the door. My heart and chest are hurting more and more the farther I get from the door. I get into the truck, and I turn off everything. Or at least I try, but nothing, nothing helps this time. I should be good at this; I should be able to do this.

When I turn off my property, the beating in my heart speeds up, and the pain hurts even more. Turning the radio on, I try to bury it deep, and when I park my truck in front of Beau's stable, my whole body screams to go back.

"What the fuck are you doing here?" Beau asks when I open the door and step out. I look over at him and see that he's wearing his workout clothes and carrying a saddle. "Didn't you just get back?"

"Yeah." I ignore the first part of his question and follow him into the barn. Beau and I have become a lot closer in the past few years, especially with our businesses crossing paths.

"If you just got back, why the fuck are you here?" he asks, throwing the saddle on one of the mustangs that he bought from me six months ago.

"We have a meeting," I say. "Did you forget?"

"I didn't forget." He looks over at me. "I assumed we would reschedule since your woman just went through hell."

I look at him. "She isn't my woman." As soon as I say the words, I feel like I just swallowed a handful of nails.

"Wow." He shakes his head. "You're really that fucking stupid." I glare at him.

"You are one to talk." I put my hands on my hips. "How is Savannah?" I ask him, and it's his turn to glare at me. "You can dish it, but can you take it?"

"It's not even the same thing," he says.

"Isn't it? You've loved her your whole life. The whole town knows it. The only one who doesn't know it is Savannah because you haven't told her." I point at him.

"You told Olivia you love her?" he asks, and I glare. "I mean, you do love her, right? You have to. There is no way you would have her in your house if you didn't. That is your place, your 'woman-free space'." He uses quotations, and I want to throat punch him, but instead, all I can do is stand here and listen to him. "If you let her walk away without telling her how you feel, you are going to regret it for the rest of your life."

"How would you know?" I say. "You are glued to Savannah's side, yet you never told her."

He looks at me. "She has a kid with my best friend." He looks down, and I know that deep down it cuts him to the core. "Besides, there is no way she would ever feel the same about me. It would just make it awkward for everyone."

"You never know until you tell her and hear what she has to say," I say, and he walks toward me now.

"Are you going to take your own advice?" he asks, and I look down.

"Her whole life is in Los Angeles." My heart skips a beat. "Her whole life is nothing like I can give her here."

"Maybe all she wants is you, dumb ass," he says, laughing. "By the way, I'm canceling our meeting right now." He turns and walks back to his horse and gets on it. "Go home and take your head out of your ass," he says as he nudges his horse to ride. I watch him longer than I want to, and the whole time, my head is going around and around.

When I finally open the front door and walk into my house, I stop when I walk past her room and hear her. I turn to walk to her and see her turning to the closet and grabbing her stuff. My feet are stuck to the floor. I watch her walk back and forth to the suitcase twice before I notice that her face looks like she's been crying. I stand here not able to say anything, wondering if she heard about Dominic and that is the reason she is crying.

"What are you doing?" The words finally come out. She jumps at the sound of my voice, and I see right away that she has a shield up. Her eyes are clouded over, and her smile is fake as fuck.

"Well," she says, trying to sound upbeat, "I figured that

you needed me out of your hair." She puts the clothes into the suitcase, and I want to walk up to it and take them out. But not replace it in the drawers in this room. I want it in my room and the thought of her leaving is too much to bear. "I've been cramping your style for far too long." She avoids my eyes. "I'm going to go and stay at Kallie's house for now until I figure it out."

"Until you figure out what?" I ask her, stepping into the room, the whole time my hands itch to grab her.

She drops the clothes into the suitcase and then looks up at me. "Until I figure out where the next step is." I look at her up and down and notice that she changed from her dress and is now wearing shorts and a sweater. "One thing I've decided is that it's not LA." It's almost as if she kicks me in the balls with that last sentence, but then it's nothing like the next part. "It's not my home." She turns and walks back to the closet and grabs a handful of hangers. "I want to find a home." She smiles sadly. "With everything that happened around me, I figured one thing out. I've never had a home. I've never had roots. I want to build a home and then plant all the roots."

"Darlin'." I say her name softly, and she blinks and looks down, but I can't stop staring at the lone tear that rolls down her cheek.

"I know you won't get it because you've had a home your whole life," she says, taking the shirt off the hanger and then looking up at me. "So you probably think it's silly, but ..." She shrugs. "I want a home." Her eyes glisten with tears. "I want a family that is my own. I want to bake and cook for them." She laughs now. "I mean, I have to learn, but still. I want to."

"Stay," I finally say, my tongue finally working, and she looks at me. "Stay here."

"What?" she whispers, and I take a step closer to her. "And I know that I said I didn't know what love was or that I didn't deserve it or the fact that I don't want to have kids but ..." She shrugs, looking at me almost in defeat. "But I am worthy of love. I'm worthy of loving someone, and I'm worthy of someone loving me. I want to be a mother and a wife. I want all those things and more. You said yourself that you'll never get married." She reminds me of the words I told her, and I suddenly want to go back to that day by the creek and take it back. But I can't touch her yet. I need to get this off my chest before I touch her.

"That was then," I say. "That was before I knew how much I want to be married. I'm saying that because I want you to stay here with me. You once asked me about the room upstairs. Why I built it." I take one more step. "And I told you I did it for my nieces and nephews, and I never said I did it for my kids, and the reason was because I was never going to get married." I watch her as she processes what I just said. "I was never going to let myself get serious with someone. It was easier." I take another step. "And then I met you." My heart is beating. "I met you, and everything that I thought went straight out the window."

"Casey," she says, shaking her head and now a sob rips out of her.

"I watched you sleep last night," I say. "I watched your chest rise and fall, and the whole time I told myself I wasn't going to tell you how I felt because I didn't want to pressure you into staying." The tears that run down her face flow faster now. "I didn't think I was good enough, or that I had what you needed. I didn't have anything to offer you. I don't even know if I have what you need or want but ..." I shake my head, blinking away my own tears. "I want to build this home with you. I want to help you plant those roots, and if you don't like it here, we can plant the roots wherever you want. The only thing I know is that you are the only one I want to do this with."

"Casey," she whispers again, and this time, I close the

space between us, and I'm standing in front of her. I take the hanger out of her hand and toss it on the bed. She puts her hands to her face and sobs. I pull them from her face.

"I love you." I finally say three words I've never said to anyone in my whole life, not counting my family. "I love you so much." Her eyes light up. "All of you."

"Cowboy," she says, hanging her head and coming into my arms and crying in my neck. My arms wrap around her, and for the first time today, my heart beats properly. Like it's found its missing piece.

I kiss the top of her head. "Don't cry, darlin'," I say, hugging her even tighter.

"I thought you wanted me gone," she finally says softly. "You wouldn't look at me this morning." She doesn't move her face from the crook of my neck. "I thought you were disgusted by me."

"What?" I shriek out and push her away from me so she can see my face. "How can you think that?"

"You wouldn't even look at me," she says softly, avoiding my eyes, and I put my finger under her chin so I can see her, and she can see me. "I just ..."

"I left because I couldn't stand the thought of you wanting to leave. I left because I couldn't imagine you not here."

"Well, that was dumb, cowboy," she says and smiles. "I love you." Her whole face lights up, and I see her shield is down, and that she is bursting. "I have never loved anyone like I love you. I didn't think I was good enough for you," she says. "I didn't think you would want to settle with someone who has never had a family." She wrings her hands together. "Someone who has such a dark cloud over her head."

"You have more than you know, Olivia," I say. "You are more than I deserve."

"Ask me again?" she says, and I finally smile for the first time today.

"Stay with me." I don't really ask her. "Build a home with me."

She looks down at her hands, and when she looks up, she smiles so big her eyes look like she's squinting. "Yes."

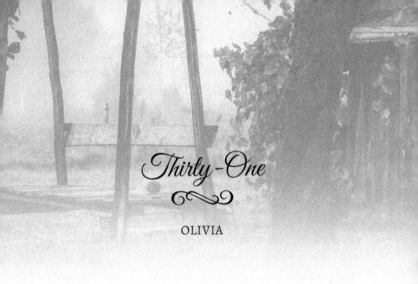

Thirty-One

OLIVIA

"Why are we doing this again?" Casey asks from beside me, and I shake my head and try not to laugh.

"We are doing this because Beau is one of your good friends, and he invited us over to help celebrate him winning the mayor's seat," I say, leaning over and kissing his cheek. It's been one month since he asked me to stay and build a home with him. It's also been a month since my dreams have come true. I called Meryl and was about to quit my job. I didn't give a shit, but she just gave me the same deal she gave Kallie when she called her. When Casey found out, he called Kallie, and they redid the office exactly like it was at home. I was so overwhelmed that I thanked him right there on the desk.

"But I thanked him already." Casey moans, and I look over at him. I forced him to wear slacks today, and you would think I asked him to pull out his wisdom teeth. He looked over at me and gave me a list of sexual positions we would have to do in order for him to dress like that. I rolled my eyes the whole time, but little did he know that I was probably more excited than he was.

When we get to the big mayor's house, two men in

tuxedos wait for us. One opens my door and the other runs to the other side and opens Casey's. I step out and my heels click on the sidewalk as I wait for Casey to come around the truck. He grabs my hand and then kisses me silly right here in the middle of the sidewalk while people arrive. "I hate when you wear pants," he says, and I look down at my white capri pants I wore for the night with my one-sleeved black shirt. "It just takes longer to do you when we get home."

I shake my head. "Since when are pants an issue with you?" I ask him while we walk up the walkway. "Two days ago, I wore yoga pants at breakfast." I smile, thinking back of how he just peeled off one leg and just left the other leg covered.

"That was not my fault." He smirks at me. "You bent over."

"To get a fork I dropped." I throw my head back and laugh. "It was not an invitation."

He shrugs when we walk up the five steps, and the door is opened for us. It's an old Victorian house with the American flag hanging beside the front door. "Welcome."

"Thank you," I say, walking in and seeing the high ceiling with a crystal chandelier. "This is beautiful," I say, taking in all the old Victorian touches everywhere. The spiral staircase on the side of the room, and the pictures of the family all along them. "Do they really live here?"

"If you are mayor, you live here," Casey says from beside me. "So he has no choice but to move in here, no matter how much he bitches."

"But doesn't his father live here?" I look over at him and spot servers walking around with champagne on trays. I take a glass and look back at Casey. "Awkward giving your father the pink slip to move out."

"It's about time," Casey says, and then we walk past the room on the right that has the mayor's office on the closed door. "We need new blood."

I don't have a chance to ask him what he means when we come into the big open room that leads out to the huge backyard. Where over a hundred people all stand mingling with each other. I spot Beau standing next to his father and then look next to him and see someone else. "Who is that?" I ask Casey, pointing.

"That's Liam, Beau's brother," he says, leaning in. "He's also a fucking tool." I shake my head as we walk out onto the back patio, and I spot Kallie and Jacob with Ethan standing on one side.

"Look at how pretty the willow tree is," I say, pointing at the tree and then turning to smile at Kallie, who is dressed in a pencil skirt with a button-down shirt. "Hello, everyone."

"Hello, yourself," Kallie says. "What took you so long?"

I shrug my shoulder and take a sip of the champagne, not getting into the real reason we are late. I'm sure she doesn't want to know it was because her brother tore off another pair of panties and had his way with me. "I didn't know what to wear."

"This is something, right?" Jacob says, shaking his head. "I bet you Beau fucking hates this."

We all look over at him and see that he's pulling the shirt from around his neck. "Can I go to the swing?" Ethan asks. Jacob nods his head, and we watch him run away.

"How long do we have to stay?" Casey asks, and I groan and then the chatter around us stops and we all look toward the door where Savannah stands. "Jesus, even eight years later, people still fucking point." I watch her as she looks around, and you can see she's not happy to be here. She is wearing a tight red dress that goes all the way to her neck and is tight all the way down to her knees, and then it ruffles off. It's a stunning dress she's paired with black heels. Her eyes find Beau's, and she smiles huge. You can see how much she loves him, but the only one who doesn't know is him.

I follow her eyes to Beau's, who smiles just as big, and when he sees her, he finally walks away from his brother and his father, who both glare at her. He weaves his way to her, and when she finally comes down the steps, he hugs her and kisses her cheek. They make their way over to us, and we all smile at him.

"There he is, Mr. Mayor," Kallie says, joking with him, and he shakes his head. "Do you curtsey to a mayor?"

"There is no fucking way in hell I'll ever curtsey to him," Jacob says. "He keeps eating all the fucking food in my fridge."

"It's not my fault," Beau says. "You always invite me over."

"I never invite you over," Jacob says.

"Who wants to see the major's office?" Beau says, and the guys all nod. Jacob kisses Kallie, and Casey leans over to kiss me, and the three of them leave.

"Am I missing something?" I ask as the men walk up the steps and enter the house.

"The guys used to sneak into the office when they were younger and take some of Mr. Beaumont's whiskey," Kallie says, and I laugh and so does Savannah.

"Where is Ethan?" Savannah asks, and Kallie points at the swing. I don't know how Kallie does this. Stands there with Savannah after everything they went through. But Kallie is the bigger person, and in the end, if she was bitter, it would fall onto Ethan, and she loves that kid like he's her own. "I think I'm going to vomit," she says and puts her hand to her stomach, and Kallie walks over to her and rubs her arm. "If it was for anyone else, there was no way I would come here."

"We all feel that way," Kallie says, and then I look down.

"What do you guys say we join the boys?" I smile, and the girls nod.

We walk to the house and up the steps. "I don't think a girl has ever been invited into the office for drinks," Savannah says, and when we get to the closed door, she puts her hand up to knock, and then she opens it and walks in.

The minute I step foot inside, I know something is off. I look around the office, and I spot Casey and Jacob standing there in front of the desk but neither of them is moving. The look of pure anguish is all over Jacob's face. But nothing, and I mean nothing, could prepare me for the look on Beau's face.

He has tears running down his face, and the pain in his eyes is so transparent that you feel it in your soul. The white paper in his hand crinkles as his body shakes. He looks at us standing in the door, and then he looks straight at Savannah.

"Tell me," he says almost in a whisper, then looks down at the paper in his hand. "Tell me that my brother is not the father of your son."

Epilogue One

CASEY

One Year Later

"But why?" she moans as she comes out of the bedroom, and I look over at her. She is wearing white jeans and one of my T-shirts, her feet bare, her face free of makeup. "I thought we were going to stay in tonight, and you know ..."

"It's our anniversary," I remind her, shaking my head and also wondering why I'm surprised that she would opt to stay in rather than go out on the town. I waited every single day for her to tell me that she was done with the country and wanted to move to the city. But as the days turned into weeks and then the weeks into months, she just got more and more settled.

The house that I built is now a home with her touches in every single room. The throw pillows on the couch along with the big throw blanket that we cuddle under. The pictures of the family all over the fridge. The fresh flowers in the middle of the island. The pictures of us all around the house, whether it's on the side tables or hanging on the walls. It shows that this is our home. "But." She looks at me. "I cooked for you." I look at her, and my eyebrows pinch together. She has been trying to learn the whole time. My mother by her side each and every time, but no matter what she did, she usually burnt it. "Okay, fine, I tried, and well, your mother made an extra one." I laugh now and walk to her.

"How am I supposed to wine and dine you if you won't let me?" I take her in my arms, and in a second, she has her legs wrapped around me.

She clings to me like a monkey, burrowing her face into my neck. "I don't want to be wined and dined," she whispers. "I want to be home and naked."

"I can help you with that," I say, carrying her into our room. She starts to kiss my neck, and my cock is already ready to play. Every single time I'm with her, it's like the first time. Every single time that I think it can't get better, it does. Even when I took her to Mexico and had her every single hour we were there. The private house on the beach. I rented our own oasis, and I didn't think we would top that. "You really are going to talk me out of going out tonight."

She unclings herself from me and stands in front of me. Peeling off her shirt, she shows me a new bra that I've never seen before. Trust me, I know. I've had to replace more than my share, that and her flimsy panties. "I was hoping that." She winks at me, and then she unbuttons her jeans, and I see that she has the matching panties.

I pick up my hand. "Wait," I say, and she stops mid-zip. "Jesus, I can't believe you're making me do this here," I say. Turning around and walking to my closet, I find the suit jacket I was going to wear tonight and grab the square box. I look around the closet at our stuff. When I walk back into the room, she is still there in the middle of the room. "We are going to have to make up a story."

"What in the world are you talking about?" she asks, confused. Then I get down on one knee, and it all clicks into place. I wait for it, and there it is. My girl has her hand on her mouth, and tears already running down her face.

"Olivia," I start to say. "Darlin'." I see her smile. "I never thought that this moment would come, yet after being with you for this long, I wonder why I didn't do it sooner." My own tears come now. "One year ago, I asked you to stay and make a home with me. I promised to help you plant roots. I held my breath the whole time, waiting for your answer. You didn't just help me make a home, but you also became my home."

"Casey," she says, laughing and crying at the same time.

"I built this house, not knowing that I wanted to fill it with children. I want our kids to run in from the barn and mess up the floor. I want our kids to hide in the room upstairs and then pretend they ran away. I want our kids to grow up here, and then I want them to bring their own kids here." She sobs now. "There is only one person I want to do all that with, and it's you, darlin'." She doesn't say anything; all she can do is sob. "One year ago, I asked you to stay and make a home with me. Today, I'm asking you to help me fill our home. I'm asking you to hold my hand today and always." I don't finish because she grabs my face and kisses me hard. The taste of her tears on my lips.

"Yes," she whispers, her lips still on mine. "But," she says, and my heart stops in my chest as she turns around and walks to the side of the bed and takes something out of her side table. "Just so you know." She starts to say. "We are going to be filling the house sooner than you think." She holds out the white stick to me. My eyes go to the word pregnant, and then I drop the box and take the stick from her. "Casey Barnes, you are going to be the best father anyone could ask for, and I'm so happy that our children are going to have you."

I don't move from the spot still on bended knee when it

finally hits me. "How?" I ask her, the tears now leaking down my face. She laughs at me.

"If I need to tell you how?" She shakes her head.

Laughing, I grab the box that fell out of my hand and open it, and just as I know, my girl doesn't even look at the ring. She couldn't care less, but I care. So, I went overboard, and she is probably going to moan about how big it is, but I couldn't care less. She now looks down and gasps out at the five-carat pink square diamond ring that I got for her. "I know that it's not traditional, but when I saw it, the only thing I could think of was the sunsets that we watch every night. How the sky turns a light pink right before the sun sets, and I knew that it felt like home."

"Yes," she says before I say the words again and lunges for me, making me fall back.

"I love you," I say to her right before I rip off her new panties.

Epilogue Two

OLIVIA

Five Years Later

"What is all this fuss about?" I ask, walking into the nursery while my two-week-old daughter, Harlow, cries at the top of her lungs. "I just fed you," I say, taking her in my arms, and I kiss her soft cheek. The minute she is in my arms, she quiets. "Not you, too," I say to myself, walking over to the rocking chair and sitting down. "After your two brothers, we said you wouldn't be spoiled," I say, and she just closes her eyes while her hands are folded over her chest. "I'm giving you two more minutes, and then I'm going to put you back in your crib." I rock her back and forth and look around at the pink nursery. After having the boys, Quinn, who is four, and then Reed, who just turned two, I went full-on bubble gum pink for her.

I rock her for five minutes and then get up, placing her down gently. She stirs for just a moment, and then I walk back out of the room. I walk down the hall to Quinn's room, and I find him in the middle of his bed, sleeping like a starfish with the covers already thrown on the floor. My son hates to be covered, no matter how many times I try. Walking in, I turn off the light and lean over, kissing him on his cheek. He looks exactly like Casey, right down to the way he smirks at you. He is also the biggest daredevil in the world. Last week, he somehow convinced Billy to let him ride a mustang. "I love you," I whisper and walk out of the room, pulling the door closed behind me but leaving it open just a crack. I walk over to the other room and find Casey in bed with Reed. My heart stops in my chest when I see him spooning Reed. I lean down and kiss my husband's cheek, and he slowly opens his eyes. "Hey."

"Hey," he mumbles. "Is she asleep?"

"For now," I say. "I'm going to go to sleep." I lean over and kiss Reed's cheek, and he turns over right away. He also came out looking exactly like Casey, something that I resented since I carried them for nine long months.

Casey gets off the bed and turns off the light. He puts his arm around me as we walk toward our bedroom. I grab his hand that is on my shoulder, and I kiss it. His wedding band shines in the dim light. It took him three weeks to wear me down and agree to a shotgun wedding. If I'm honest, I would have married him the same day he asked me. "If you want, I can take the next feeding."

"No," I say softly. "It's fine." I didn't know what type of mom I was going to be. I mean, I had an idea of what type of mother I wanted to be, but I didn't know I would be that type of mom. The mom who didn't let her kids do anything unless I was there. The mom who spent all her waking time with them, the mom who would make five different dinners just so they would eat. I'm the pushover mom, the mom who says no, but really, it's a yes.

"You're tired, and if you don't get the rest you need," he says, "you are going to get sick."

"I know," I say. I pushed myself after we came home with

Harlow, and within four days, I was in the hospital after faint-ing. "Fine, you can feed her," I say. "There is a bottle in the fridge."

He gets into the bed, and when I slide in with him, he quickly finds me and pulls me to him. "I love you, darlin'," he says softly, and I kiss him. The kissing quickly takes on a life of its own, making us itch for more, but we still have another four weeks to go. "Fuck," he whispers, and I know that it's killing him. "I thought six weeks would have been easier the third time around."

I laugh into his neck, and I close my eyes. It takes maybe three minutes before I fall asleep.

I wake up when my breasts start to hurt, and when I look over, I see that the spot next to me is empty. I turn and look at the clock, and it shows that it's a little bit after midnight. I've been sleeping for four glorious hours. I'm about to get up and find Casey when I hear him in the monitor and look over to see the image of him rocking Harlow on the screen.

"I know you don't like the bottle, Princess H." He talks to her. "But Momma needs her rest."

The sounds of her little cry fill the room now. "I have the goods right here. All you have to do is take it. That's it, my girl." I wipe the tear that is now rolling down the side of my face. I didn't know that someone could be this happy. I didn't know that I could love someone so deeply that I can't exist without them. I didn't know that my biggest nightmare would be my fairy-tale ending.

I watch the two of them the whole time, my eyes never leaving them, and when he puts our daughter on his chest, I can't stop the tears from coming. I can't stop these over-whelming feelings, and when he comes into the room five minutes later and takes me in his arms, the only thing I can do is whisper, "Thank you for giving me my home."

He kisses my lips. "Thank you for filling my home."

Books By Natasha Madison

Southern Wedding Series
Mine To Have
Mine To Hold
Mine To Cherish
Mine To Love

The Only One Series
Only One Kiss
Only One Chance
Only One Night
Only One Touch
Only One Regret
Only One Moment
Only One Love
Only One Forever

Southern Series
Southern Chance
Southern Comfort
Southern Storm
Southern Sunrise
Southern Heart
Southern Heat
Southern Secrets
Southern Sunshine

This Is
This Is Crazy
This Is Wild
This Is Love
This Is Forever

Hollywood Royalty
Hollywood Playboy

BOOKS BY NATASHA MADISON

Hollywood Princess
Hollywood Prince

Something Series
Something So Right
Something So Perfect
Something So Irresistible
Something So Unscripted
Something So BOX SET

Tempt Series
Tempt The Boss
Tempt The Playboy
Tempt The Hookup

Heaven & Hell Series
Hell and Back
Pieces of Heaven
Heaven & Hell Box Set

Love Series
Perfect Love Story
Unexpected Love Story
Broken Love Story

Mixed Up Love
Faux Pas

Printed in the USA
CPSIA information can be obtained
at www.ICGtesting.com
LVHW092249280324
775804LV00031B/652